The Kitten Nobody Wanted

and other tales

The Kitten Nobody Wanted

and other tales

by Holly Webb

Illustrated by Sophy Williams

tiger tales

tiger tales

5 River Road, Suite 128, Wilton, CT 06897
Published in the United States 2016
Text copyright © Holly Webb
The Kitten Nobody Wanted 2011
The Frightened Kitten 2012
The Stray Kitten originally published as *Ginger the Stray Kitten* 2009
Illustrations copyright © Sophy Williams
The Kitten Nobody Wanted 2011
The Frightened Kitten 2012
The Stray Kitten originally published as *Ginger the Stray Kitten* 2009
ISBN-13: 978-1-68010-405-9
ISBN-10: 1-68010-405-5
Printed in China
STP/1000/0119/0716

For more insight and activities, visit us at www.tigertalesbooks.com

Contents

The Kitten Nobody Wanted

Contents

For everyone remembering a much-missed cat

Chapter One
Missing Sandy

"Oh, Mia, look! I told you Mrs. Johnston had a new cat. Isn't she beautiful? So fluffy!" Mia's mom stroked the little black cat, who was sitting proudly on Mrs. Johnston's front wall.

Mia's best friend, Emily, tickled the purring cat under the chin. "She's so pretty!"

Mia's mom looked over at Mia hopefully, then sighed. She hadn't even glanced up as Mom and Emily petted the cat. She was staring firmly at her school shoes as she marched on down the road. It was as if she hadn't heard.

Mom and Emily exchanged worried looks and hurried after her. Emily lived a few houses down from Mia, and the girls usually walked to school together. Their moms and Mia's grandma took turns going with them, now that Emily's big sister, Leah, had started high school. Grandma lived in a couple of downstairs rooms in Mia's house and took care of Mia when her parents were working. She'd moved in with them a few years ago, when she'd been sick and it had been difficult for her to live on her own.

12

"See you tomorrow, Mia!" Emily called as she turned into her yard.

"'Bye! Call me if you get stuck on that homework!" Mia was very good at math, and Emily wasn't. Emily had been complaining about their math homework all the way back from school.

Mia flung off her coat and hurried upstairs before Mom could start going on about Mrs. Johnston's gorgeous cat again. She could hear her mom asking her if she was okay, if she wanted a drink, but she ignored her.

Mia just didn't want to hear. She'd never realized before how many cats there were in her neighborhood, or on the way to school. Now that she couldn't bear to see them, there seemed to be cats everywhere.

She slumped down on her bed, and looked sadly at the navy blue fleece blanket spread over her comforter at the end. It had a pattern of little cat faces scattered on it—and there were still orange hairs clinging to it here and there. Sandy had slept on it every night, for as long as Mia could remember. She still woke up in the middle of the night expecting her old cat to be there—sometimes she even reached down to pet him, waiting for his sleepy purr as he felt her move. It was so hard to believe that he was really gone.

She looked at the photo on her windowsill. It had been taken a couple of months earlier, at the beginning of summer vacation, just a few weeks before Sandy died. He was looking thin, and they'd taken him to the vet, but that day he'd been enjoying the late summer sun in the yard, and Mia had been sure he was getting better. Looking back now, she realized that he hadn't been jumping and pouncing and chasing the butterflies like he usually did, just lying quietly in the sun. But she hadn't wanted to believe that there was anything wrong with him.

Tears stung her eyes as she stroked the glass over the photo, wishing she had the real Sandy snuggled up on her lap.

How could Mom keep pointing out other cats, and expecting her to want to stop and pet them? Dad had even suggested going to the cat rescue shelter to look for a kitten! Mia didn't want a kitten, ever. She was never going to replace her beautiful Sandy.

Mom was calling her from downstairs, asking if she wanted a snack. Brushing the tears away, Mia carefully straightened Sandy's blanket, and went down to the kitchen.

16

She could tell that Mom was watching her worriedly as she ate her apple. It only made her feel worse.

"Should I go and fill up the bird feeder?" Mia asked, wanting an excuse to leave the room. Mia knew Mom was only trying to help, but she really wasn't, and any minute now she was going to start talking about kittens again, or getting a rabbit, like she'd suggested yesterday.

Mia grabbed the bag of bird food from the cupboard and let herself out of the back door, taking a deep breath of relief. A blackbird skittered out of her way as she went over to refill the feeder, and she whispered to it soothingly as she unhooked the wire case.

17

"It's all right. I'll be gone in a minute. And I'll probably drop pieces, so you can peck them up." She poured in the seed, and then hung up the feeder and perched on the arm of the bench, shivering a little in the autumn sun. She didn't want to go back inside just yet.

All of a sudden, a damp nose butted her hand and Mia jumped, a strange, silly hope flooding into her.

But when she turned around, it wasn't her beautiful Sandy playing tricks on her. It was a pretty, plump white cat with blue eyes, and Mia recognized her: Snowball, her friend Emily's cat.

"Hi, Snowball," she whispered. "You look a bit round, kitty. Emily needs to stop giving you so many treats."

18

Snowball rubbed up against her affectionately. Cats always liked Mia, and Snowball knew her anyway, as Mia spent lots of time at Emily's house. Sandy had known Emily, too, although he'd always chased Snowball if she came into his yard.

This yard.

Mia swallowed and gently pushed Snowball away, then walked quickly back into the house.

Her mom was standing by the kitchen window—she'd been watching, and she sighed, very quietly, as Mia hurried back inside.

"Are you okay, sweetheart?" she asked.

"I'm going to do my homework," Mia muttered, trying not to sound tearful. She was so sick of people worrying about her. Dad had talked to her forever at breakfast that morning about Sandy. But she was perfectly all right! Why couldn't everyone just leave her alone?

Chapter Two
The News About Snowball

Mia and her grandma called to Emily on their way to school the next morning. Emily waved at them through the front window as they walked up, and then she disappeared and flung open the door.

"Guess what!" Emily shrieked.

Mia shook her head, laughing, as Emily came running down the path.

"What? You finished the math homework and it was easy?"

Emily shuddered and made a face. "No, it was awful. I don't even want to think about it. I'll have to tell you— you'll never guess. We think Snowball is going to have kittens!"

Grandma smiled delightedly, and Mia gasped. "What, really? Kittens? When will she have them?"

"We're not quite sure. Mom's going to take her to the vet today to check. We were looking at her last night, and we just realized how big she'd gotten around the middle! Mom's a little annoyed, though. Well, she's excited, but she says it's going to be a big pain, and we'll have to find homes for all the kittens." Emily frowned. "But Leah and I are going to work on Mom to let us keep one of them."

"Oh, wow…," Mia muttered. "You know, Snowball came into our yard yesterday, and I thought she was looking a little plump. But I didn't realize she was having kittens!" *I only looked at her for a minute before I pushed her away*, Mia thought, feeling guilty.

Emily chattered on happily about the kittens all the way to school, wondering how many there would be, and whether they'd be white like Snowball.

Mia joined in with a comment here and there, but thoughts were buzzing around inside her head. She still loved cats, of course she did. But it was definitely hard to be around them right now, when every cat seemed to remind her so much of Sandy. It wouldn't be so difficult if her mom and dad weren't so anxious for them to get another pet—they seemed to think Mia needed another cat to get over Sandy. And now Emily was all excited about kittens as well....

"What's the matter, Mia? You're so quiet," Emily asked, as they waved to Grandma and went in through the school gates.

Mia smiled and shook her head. "I'm fine. I'm glad I'm walking home with you and my mom today—can we stop in and see Snowball, and ask your mom what the vet said?" She was trying hard to sound excited, like she knew she should, and it must have worked, because Emily beamed at her.

"Of course you can!" Emily said, giving her a hug. "I can't wait to tell everyone about Snowball having kittens! I just hope it's true!"

Emily told Mia's mom the news as soon as they came out of school. She'd come right from work to pick them up and hadn't spoken to Grandma, so it was a total surprise.

"Oh, Mia, isn't that wonderful? Kittens!"

"Mmm." Mia tried to sound enthusiastic. She really didn't want to spoil things for Emily. "Can we see Snowball on the way home?"she asked. "Emily's mom took Snowball to the vet, so she should know for certain by now—maybe she'll even know when the kittens might be born."

Mom nodded. "Of course!"

They hurried back to Emily's house, and Emily burst through the door, racing ahead and calling for her mom. "What did the vet say? Is she definitely having kittens? When will they come?"

"Sooner than we thought!" her mom said, laughing. "Could be only a couple of weeks, the vet said. And she felt Snowball's tummy, and she thinks there are at least three kittens, possibly more."

"Three!" Emily breathed, crouching down next to Snowball, who was curled up in her furry basket. "That explains why she's so fat!"

Mia sat down next to her friend and petted Snowball gently. Her fur was beautifully soft and smooth. She wasn't asleep, but her pretty blue eyes were half-closed, as though she was tired. *She probably is*, Mia thought.

27

"Three kittens to find homes for," her mom sighed. She looked thoughtfully at Mia's mom. "I don't suppose...?"

Mia saw her mom smile, and glance over at her, raising her eyebrows. Emily's mom glanced at her, too, and nodded understandingly. Mia could tell exactly what Mom meant—*Maybe, but I'm not sure about Mia.*

She gave Snowball one last gentle pet. It was odd to think that there were tiny kittens squirming around inside her.

"Mom, I've got a ton of homework," she pointed out, getting to her feet. "We'd better go." They didn't really need to leave that minute, but she didn't want her mom and Emily's mom exchanging any more of those secret looks.

The subject didn't go away, though. Dad was full of questions at dinnertime, wanting to know when the kittens would arrive, and what Snowball had looked like.

"Snowball's such a sweet cat," he said, looking at Mia. "She'll have cute kittens, Mia, don't you think?"

Mia nodded. "But they won't be as beautiful as Sandy," she said, eyeing her dad firmly. "We'll never find another cat like him."

He shook his head with a sigh. "No, I suppose not. But different can be good, too, you know, Mia."

When she went up to bed that night, Mia lay there for a while, hugging Sandy's blanket and thinking. She'd never actually had a kitten of her own. Sandy had been older than she was; he was about two when she was born. Grandma had a photo of him that she kept in her living room, one that Mom and Dad had sent her when she still lived in her old house, before she came to live with them all a few years later. It was a photo of Mia as a baby, sitting up in her bouncy chair, and reaching out a fat little hand for Sandy's tail as he strolled past.

Mom had photos of Sandy as a kitten, too, in her photo album. He'd been super cute—with round green eyes that looked too big for his little whiskery face, and pink pads on his paws. They were darker by the time Mia knew him, from going outside and roughening them up. But he was still beautiful, and his eyes were like emeralds.

Mia gulped and buried her face in the blanket. It still smelled like him. She really wanted to be excited for Emily, but even the thought of kittens made her miss Sandy so much. She wasn't sure she could bear to see them for real.

Chapter Three
A Difficult Time

"I wonder if there's any news yet!" Emily said excitedly as they put on their coats at the end of school. "Mom's picking us up today. I can't wait to ask her. Snowball has been a little shy and weird all weekend, then she went off and snuggled herself up in the hall closet this morning. I'm sure that means she's 'nesting,' getting ready for her kittens to come."

It was Monday, two weeks since Emily had found out Snowball was having kittens, and she had been getting more and more impatient every day.

Mia smiled. Even though the thought of kittens made her miss Sandy, she could see how happy Emily was. They hurried out onto the playground, looking eagerly for Emily's mom. But she wasn't there. Instead, Mia's grandma was waving at them from the gate.

"Grandma! What are you doing here?" Mia called in surprise.

Grandma smiled. "Snowball is having her kittens! Your mom didn't want to leave her on her own, Emily, so she called me. My legs aren't too bad today, so I was glad to come out for a walk."

"She's having them right now?" Emily squealed in delight, whirling her schoolbag around. "Ooooh, how many are there?"

"Four so far, apparently, and your mom thought that might be it, but she wasn't sure."

"Four kittens!" Emily said blissfully, and even Mia felt her stomach squirm with excitement. "Can Mia come in and see them, Mrs. Lovett?" Emily asked Mia's grandma.

"Better not today," Grandma said thoughtfully. "They've only just been born, and Snowball will be tired and very protective of her new babies, I would think. She won't want visitors. You can tell Mia about them tomorrow."

Emily walked home so fast she was practically running, and she dashed into her yard with a wave, leaving Mia and her grandma to walk to their house.

"You're looking serious, Mia," Grandma commented. "Aren't you excited about the kittens?"

Mia was silent for a moment. The walk home and Emily's happy chattering about Snowball's babies had brought back that strange, miserable feeling again, even worse than before. It seemed so unfair that Emily should have her beautiful Snowball and four adorable little kittens, too. She wasn't jealous of Emily, exactly—just sad.

"I was," she admitted. "When you told us they were coming, I thought it was wonderful. But then Emily started

36

talking about how sweet they'd be, and how she was looking forward to cuddling them and playing with them. And it just made me miss Sandy so much!" She leaned her face against Grandma's arm. "I'm not even sure I want to go and see them," she whispered.

Grandma nodded thoughtfully. "I wondered if that was it. Poor Mia." She gave her a hug as they reached their driveway. "Come on. Let's go and make some hot chocolate. Maybe that will cheer you up a little."

Emily was full of news of the kittens the next day at school. Their friends Lisa and Anna rushed up to her, desperate to know what had happened. Mia did her best to join in and sound enthusiastic, but it was hard.

"There's a black one, and two tabbies, and the last one to be born was a tiny, tiny little white one, with the most enormous set of whiskers!" Emily beamed at Mia. "Do you think you can come and see them after school?"

Mia hesitated. She could—but she was worried she'd do something awful like start crying. "Um, I'm not sure," she said slowly. "Grandma's picking me up, and she said something about going shopping."

"Oh." Emily looked a bit surprised, as though she'd been expecting Mia to be more excited, and Mia felt guilty.

"Did you learn those spelling words?" she asked quickly, to try and distract Emily from the kittens.

Emily made a face. "Well, I looked at them. But the kittens were so fun to watch. They're all just nosing around each other and Snowball and squeaking. It's so funny! I probably haven't learned them correctly." She sighed. "Can you test me?"

Mia nodded, feeling relieved. She'd gotten away with it for today, but she wasn't going to be able to keep on making excuses. Sooner or later, she was going to have to go and see the kittens.

By the end of the week, Mia had run out of excuses to say to Emily, and Emily was running out of patience. On Friday at lunchtime, she told Mia that her mom said she could come over on the weekend to see the kittens if she wanted.

Mia's mind went blank. What could she possibly say, except that she didn't want to? She couldn't pretend to be busy for the entire weekend.

"So will you come?" Emily asked, staring at her and frowning slightly.

Mia opened her mouth, and then closed it again helplessly.

"You don't want to, do you?" Emily said. Her voice was flat, and Mia could see that she was really hurt. It made Mia feel terrible.

"Sorry," she whispered.

"Is it because of Sandy?" Emily said. She sounded like she was trying to be angry, but she couldn't manage it. Emily was terrible at arguing. When she and Mia had a fight, it usually only lasted two minutes before Emily cried.

Mia nodded. "It's not that I don't want you to have them. I just miss Sandy, and you having all those kittens...."

"I know you miss Sandy," Emily said, her voice getting shaky already.

"But you're supposed to be my best friend, and you should at least try to be happy for me! I really wanted to show them to you."

Mia nodded. She felt like she might cry now, too. "I know! I really am trying! I just can't make myself stop being sad about him. I can't be happy about the kittens. I can't do it!"

Emily stared back at her, tears welling up in her brown eyes, and then she gave a huge sniff and raced off to hide in the corner of the playground behind one of the benches.

Mia stared after her sadly. She knew she should go after her friend and say she was sorry, and promise that of course she'd go and see the kittens. But her feet just wouldn't move.

It was a very strange walk home. Mia and Emily didn't talk to each other, and Mia's grandma, who'd come to pick them up, could hardly get them to talk to her, either. For Mia, it was a relief when Emily ducked into her yard.

43

"What on earth's the matter?" Grandma asked as they took off their coats in the hallway. "Did you two have a fight?"

"Sort of…," Mia admitted.

"Well, I hope you're going to make up soon, Mia. You both looked so miserable. Can't you talk to her about it? Why don't you give her a call?"

Mia shook her head. "It wasn't really that sort of fight. We didn't yell at each other, or anything. It's mostly my fault, and Emily won't be my friend unless I can figure it out. But I can't…." She sniffed. She'd spent the entire afternoon feeling awful, and now that she was home with only Grandma to see, she felt like just letting herself cry.

Grandma hugged her. "Oh, Mia.

44

Why don't you tell me? Maybe talking to someone else will help."

Mia shook her head. "I don't think it will," she whispered. But she let Grandma lead her into her little living room, and sat down on the sofa with her.

Grandma gave her a tissue. "Go on, Mia. What happened?"

"She wants me to go and see her kittens."

"And you can't?"

Mia leaned against her shoulder. "It makes me too sad," she whispered. "Mom and Dad keep talking about us getting another pet, a rabbit, or even another cat. It's like everyone's forgotten Sandy."

Grandma sighed. "I don't think that's true, Mia. Your mom and dad are trying to cheer you up, that's all. We all loved Sandy, you know that. He was your special cat, though. I do understand."

"I really, really miss him...," Mia said tearfully. "Mom and Dad won't listen to me. They think I should have gotten over it by now, and I'm just being silly!"

"Oh, Mia, they really don't think that. They just want you to be happy."

"But it was August when he died, and it's only October now. I haven't stopped missing him yet." Mia sniffed. "I can't imagine not missing him! And now I can't even say anything about it to Emily, because she's so excited about her kittens. I tried to explain, but she didn't understand."

"It's such a special time for her,"

Grandma said, stroking Mia's hair. "She can't help being happy about it, can she?"

"I guess not. I just wish I could be happy with her, that's all."

"Are you sure you want to be happy?" Grandma said thoughtfully, and Mia sat up and stared at her.

"Of course I am! I don't want to be miserable!"

"But I think you're hanging onto being sad, Mia. At least if you're miserable, someone's still missing Sandy. It's as if he's still here. Do you see what I mean?"

Mia shook her head. "It isn't like that...." But her voice trailed off. Maybe it was, a little bit.

"Look." Grandma got up, and picked up a small photo album from a shelf.

"I've been making this for you, Mia, but I wasn't going to give it to you yet, in case it just made you more upset."

"Oh, Grandma! All these photos of Sandy...." Mia turned the pages, laughing as Sandy turned from a little orange fluffball into the big, handsome cat she remembered. "He was so special," she said sadly.

"Do you know what I noticed most of all about these photos?" Grandma asked, smiling at a picture of Sandy last Christmas, lying in a pile of wrapping paper, a ribbon wrapped around his paws. "He was always such a happy cat."

Mia smiled. It was true.

"Except those last couple of weeks, when he was sick. He was so tired that he wasn't really himself anymore. He'd purr if we petted him, especially for you. But most of the time, he just slept."

Mia nodded. "He didn't even want to eat."

"Exactly. And this was Sandy—he loved his food!"

Mia giggled. Mom was always getting angry with Sandy—if she left anything lying around in the kitchen while she

49

was cooking, she only had to turn her back for a second, and a sneaky orange paw would have swiped it. He even ate mushrooms, which was very unusual for a cat.

"He wasn't happy, was he?" she muttered.

Grandma shook her head. "No. And he loved you so much, Mia. He hated it when you were miserable about something, didn't he?"

"Like that time I fell down." Mia closed her eyes, remembering. She'd fallen down the stairs and banged her arm—not actually broken it, but it had still really hurt. She'd been moping around the house with it all bandaged up, until Sandy had come and sat on her while she was lying on the sofa. He sat on her chest and stared at her, dangling his big white whiskers in her face and purring like a lawnmower. It was as though he was determined to cheer her up. And of course, it had worked!

"You're right." She turned to the last picture in the album. It was Emily and her, both holding Sandy—he was big enough for two girls to hold. They were both grinning at the camera, and Sandy looked so pleased with himself.

"Emily's your best friend, Mia. You have to make an effort for friends, even if it's hard sometimes."

Mia nodded. "I know. I'll call Emily and say I'm sorry, and I'll go and see the kittens soon. Maybe on Monday. And I'll try to stop missing Sandy so much, Grandma. I really will."

Chapter Four
Mia's New Friend

Grandma must have told Mom about the talk she'd had with Mia, because on Monday morning Mom said she'd walk Mia to school, and they'd stop and pick up Emily on the way.

"Maybe you can just pop in and see the kittens," Mom suggested. "Not for long, though, because you and Emily can't be late for school. Okay?"

Mia nodded, and gave her mom a quick hug. She could see what Mom was doing. She was giving Mia a chance to see the kittens for just a couple of minutes. If it made her too sad, they could say they had to get to school.

Emily and her mom were waiting for them at the door. Mom had probably called Emily's mom, Mia decided, feeling a sudden rush of love for Mom and Grandma, worrying about her and trying to make everything okay again. The fussing had gotten on her nerves before, but they were only being nice.

"Come and see, come and see!" Emily grabbed her. "We came down this morning and they'd opened their eyes. They're so cute!" She stopped pulling Mia along and looked at her worriedly.

"You still want to see them, don't you?"

Mia nodded. "Of course. And I'm sorry I've been such a grump."

"Oh, you weren't!" Emily hugged her.

Mia was still anxious as she followed Emily into the warm kitchen. Snowball and the kittens had a little bed that Emily's mom had made out of blankets, inside a big box. It was close to the radiator to make sure the kittens stayed warm.

"Just look at them," Emily said proudly. "Aren't they the most beautiful things you've ever seen?"

Mia glanced at the bed, and Snowball yawned hugely and stared back at her. She looked as though she agreed with Emily entirely, and she expected Mia to agree, too. There was a definite look

54

of smug pride on her pretty white face as she gazed down at her new family.

The kittens were wriggling around next to their mom. Just as Mia leaned closer, the black kitten, who seemed to be the biggest, although it was hard to tell, climbed right on top of the tiny white one, who gave an indignant squeak.

"Oh, no! Is he okay?" Mia asked anxiously, but Emily only giggled.

"I'm sure he is. They do that all the time! I wondered if it would get better when they opened their eyes, but they still just walk all over each other. And they're so greedy and pushy about getting to Snowball for their milk."

"He's the boy, isn't he? The little white one?" Emily had told Mia that they'd figured out there were three girls and one boy.

Emily nodded. "He's cute, isn't he?"

"They all are." Mia crouched down by the bed, glancing at Snowball. The white cat looked as though she was enjoying showing off her babies. The two tabby kittens were suckling, and the black one was trying to reach Snowball's side, too. But the little white kitten stayed curled up near his

56

mom's front paws. He yawned, and then gazed up at Mia with dark blue eyes.

Mia knew that he was so small he probably couldn't see her very well, but somehow he seemed to be looking right at her, and he wrinkled his nose and meowed a tiny little meow.

Mia smiled, and reached out her fingers for the kitten to sniff. How could she have thought that anything so adorable would make her sad?

Somehow after that, Mia found that the thought of the kittens didn't upset her anymore. Maybe it was because none of them was orange, like her Sandy. They were themselves instead, and although she still missed Sandy, the kittens were so cute they mostly just made her laugh. Especially the white kitten, who seemed so loving. He always nuzzled her and licked her fingers.

One Friday afternoon, a couple of weeks after the kittens were born, Mia went to play at Emily's house. She was really looking forward to it. She'd stopped over to see the kittens quite a few times since her first visit, but only quickly. Somehow, there hadn't been a

58

chance to spend enough time with the kittens.

Mia followed Emily into the kitchen. It had been two or three days since she'd seen the kittens, and she gasped as she got closer to their bed.

"They're so much bigger!"

Emily laughed. "I know! It's amazing, isn't it?"

Mia shook her head. "It's like someone's blown them up, like little furry balloons...." She crouched down to look more closely at the four kittens in their bed. One of the tabbies was stomping determinedly across the soft blankets on the floor, while the other three were feeding. "They look more cat-shaped, somehow. Do you know what I mean? They were just tiny fluffy balls before, but now they're mini-cats. Oh, look...."

The white kitten seemed to have heard her talking. He stopped feeding, and looked around curiously, trying to figure out where her voice was coming from. Then he stumbled toward her, uttering that tiny squeak of a meow that she'd heard before.

"Hello, sweetie," Mia whispered, and the kitten meowed back, trying to scramble up the side of the bed.

"Wow! He's never done that before!" Emily said, her eyes wide.

"Can I pick him up?" Mia asked hopefully. "Would Snowball mind?"

Snowball was still feeding one of the tabbies and the black kitten, but she had her head up, and she was watching Mia and the white kitten carefully.

"It should be okay, don't you think, Mom?" Emily asked. "We've picked them up before, and you can see he wants you to!"

Very gently, Mia reached into the bed and scooped up the white kitten, snuggling him carefully in her lap.

The kitten let out a little breath of a purr, padding at her school skirt with his paws. Then he curled up with a contented sigh. This was what he had wanted.

"He's so soft!" Mia whispered. "And I'm sure his whiskers have grown since I last saw him. Just look at them!"

The kitten stared up at her. He liked her voice. He recognized it from when she had come before, and the girl's smell. She had petted him, and he'd wanted her to cuddle him. He yawned and his waterfall of white whiskers shimmered.

"None of the others has whiskers like that!" Mia laughed. "You should call him Whiskers, Emily. You haven't named them yet, have you?"

Emily shook her head. She had a huge smile suddenly. "Well, we've only named the black kitten, because we're keeping her! She's going to be my birthday present!" She picked up the black kitten, who seemed to have fallen asleep while she was feeding. "I'm calling her Satin." She snuggled the kitten under her chin lovingly.

"You're so lucky!" Mia smiled, but her stomach turned over. Of course. The kittens would have to go to new owners. She sighed, and the white kitten made a little grumbling noise as his comfy lap shifted. She'd only known Whiskers—she couldn't help calling him that, even though she knew it wouldn't be his real name—for a couple of weeks, but already she knew she would miss him.

Chapter Five
The Birthday Sleepover

Whiskers wriggled himself further into the cozy fold of the blanket. He was still very tiny, but he was starting to understand more about the world, and today the world felt cold. He didn't like it. Usually he would have snuggled up next to his mother, but she had disappeared. Now that he and his sisters were a little bigger, almost four weeks old, she did that every so often.

Something soft landed in the bed next to him, and Whiskers twitched and woke out of his half-doze. It was a big, round, bright pink thing. He had no idea what it was. Neither did his two tabby sisters, who prowled toward it together, hissing fiercely. They were very good at being fierce. Whiskers and Satin watched worriedly as one of the tabby kittens dabbed a paw at the pink thing. It bounced a little. She tapped it again, and it wobbled in an interesting sort of way, so she jabbed at it with her claws out.

The balloon burst with an enormous bang, and the tabby kittens jumped back in surprise, eyeing the shriveled bit of pink that was left. Whiskers cowered in the corner of the bed, meowing with fright and wishing his mother would come. He had no idea what had happened! How had the round pink thing disappeared, and why had there been that terrible noise?

Snowball shot back into the room, convinced that someone was hurting her babies, and leaped into the bed, checking them all frantically. Whiskers pressed up against her, shivering.

"I'm sorry, kittens." Emily crouched down by the bed. "I didn't mean to scare you. It was only a balloon—I'm blowing them up for my birthday party, and that pink one must have rolled off the table."

Whiskers meowed again, eyeing the other strange round pink things he could see on the kitchen table. Did that mean there were going to be more horrible noises? When Emily tried to give him a comforting pet he let her, but he was trembling, and showing his tiny little teeth.

"Oh, no...," Emily said sadly. "It really scared you, didn't it? Well, I've got some good news. Mia's coming later, and she's staying overnight. That'll be nice, won't it? You love Mia, don't you?" She sighed to herself, almost angrily. "And Mia loves you, too. She just doesn't know it yet."

Mia had been visiting the kittens almost every day, and she always went right to Whiskers. "I wish she'd just hurry up and figure out that she should take you home," Emily told Whiskers sadly. "Mom's already talking about looking for new homes for you in a few weeks. I've given Mia lots of hints, but she doesn't get them at all, and I don't want to come out and say it in case it makes her miserable about Sandy again."

She tickled Whiskers behind the ears. "You want to be Mia's kitten, don't you, Whiskers? You never play as nicely with anyone else. And you're always sad when she goes home. You meowed after her yesterday, and you looked really lonely, even though you were cuddled up next to Snowball." She sighed. "Anyway, you'll all have to be super-cute tonight for my sleepover," she told the kittens, half-seriously. "Mia's coming, and Lisa and Anna. At least, they are if it doesn't snow before then. It's so cold now! You'd better groom your babies, Snowball. Put their party fur on!"

"Oh, did you do all the balloons, Emily? Good. I'll hang them up in the hall, and you go and get changed. Leah's just putting the birthday banner on the front door." Emily's mom hurried into the kitchen and gave her a quick hug. "Are you excited about your party?"

Emily nodded, laughing. "Of course I am. But it's so chilly! I'm not sure about sleeping on the living room floor now!"

Her mom nodded. "I know. I hope

it doesn't get too much colder before Christmas. It's still only November."

Leah came in, rubbing her fingers. "I'm frozen," she moaned, but then her eyes widened. "Hey, look at Satin!"

The black kitten was teetering on the edge of the kittens' box, and as they watched, she half-jumped, half-fell onto the kitchen floor, where she stood up and shook herself, trying to look as though she meant to do exactly that.

"Oh my goodness...," Mom muttered. "We're in for it now. They'll be everywhere. We need to remember to keep the kitchen door closed."

The two tabby kittens were now standing on their back legs, peering over the top of the box and staring at their sister with huge, round eyes, as though they couldn't believe what she'd managed to do. Satin had set off to investigate the kitchen and was sniffing thoughtfully around the table legs.

"Should I let her explore for a bit?" Emily asked, and Mom nodded.

"I think she'll wear herself out soon. Go and get changed—your friends will be here any minute. Just make sure you shut the kitchen door!"

Mia looked at the kittens a little anxiously. Lisa and Anna had just arrived, and the kitchen had suddenly gotten very noisy. She hoped Snowball and the kittens wouldn't mind.

But Satin and the two tabby kittens were loving the attention. They put on a beautiful performance of stalking a piece of yarn, and then climbed all over Lisa and Anna. Satin then snuggled up on Lisa's knee, while the tabbies fought each other for the yarn. Only Whiskers was still in the kitten bed, hiding behind Snowball.

"The little white kitten's so cute!" Anna said, reaching into the bed to pick him up. Whiskers shied away from her, but she didn't seem to notice—she grabbed him, and took him out of his safe bed, dangling him in front of her.

"Don't scare him...," Mia said worriedly. She was itching to snatch Whiskers away from Anna. It wasn't that Anna meant to frighten him; she just didn't know how to hold him correctly. But Whiskers wasn't hers. She couldn't boss Anna around. And if Mia grabbed him, he'd only be even more scared. Emily was out of the room, helping her mom put everyone's coats away, or Mia knew she'd have said something.

Anna sat down on the floor, placing Whiskers on her lap and petting him. But he was upset now, and he hissed and dug in his claws as he scrambled to get away from the loud, scary girl.

Anna squeaked. "Ow! He scratched me!" She jerked her leg, and Whiskers slipped off her lap, landing on the floor with a worried meow.

"Sshh, sshh. Come here, Whiskers." Mia stretched out a hand to him gently, and he gladly crept over to her, burrowing into her skirt as she put him on her lap.

"He didn't mean to scratch you," she told Anna. "He's just a bit more shy than the other kittens."

Anna nodded. "He's sweet, but I like the tabby ones more. They've got such

74

cute tricks! Oh,
look! That one has
yarn all wrapped around her paws!"

Mia petted Whiskers and sighed. He had cute tricks, too, like the way his huge whiskers wobbled when he yawned, and the way he always put his front paws in the food bowl, now that the kittens were starting to eat solid food. Satin and the tabbies were so much bouncier, so everyone always noticed them first.

"You need to be more friendly," she whispered to Whiskers. "You won't find an owner if you keep hiding in your bed. People will be coming to see if they want to take you home a few weeks from now. You've got to show everyone how wonderful you are."

She smiled, a little sadly. She wanted Whiskers to have a loving home of his own, but if he stayed at Emily's, it meant she'd be able to keep on seeing him. Emily's mom kept saying they were only keeping Satin, but if they couldn't find a nice owner for Whiskers, she might change her mind....

Whiskers didn't know what Mia was saying, but he liked listening to her, and she made him feel safe. He purred, very quietly, and nuzzled her hand.

"Do you want to watch the movie in our sleeping bags?" Emily asked as she took a bowl of popcorn out of the microwave. "Oh, this smells great!"

"Definitely sleeping bags," Anna agreed.

"Can we bring the kittens?" Lisa asked hopefully.

Emily's mom looked thoughtful. "I suppose, for a little while. But they'll probably want to be back with Snowball soon. And after the movie, girls, you need to go to sleep! It's getting late."

The girls all nodded angelically, but Emily winked at Mia behind her mom's back. "I've got a secret chocolate supply," she whispered. "Are you bringing Whiskers?"

Mia nodded. "If you think he won't mind. He prefers being in his bed, doesn't he?"

Emily shook her head. "Not if it's you cuddling him."

Mia's cheeks turned pink. "Do you think he likes me that much?"

Emily rolled her eyes. "Of course he does! Come on!"

Mia went into the living room, and snuggled up in her sleeping bag—even with the heat on high, it was still chilly. Emily's mom had said they'd better all sleep in a huddle to keep warm, and she'd found a bunch of extra blankets. Whiskers sat on Mia's tummy, purring quietly to himself. He was happy. He hadn't been sure about the loud girls, and people grabbing him, but now he had Mia, and she didn't seem to be going anywhere, like she usually was. He could even put up with the noisy girls if Mia was there, too.

Mia hardly paid attention to the movie at all. She was watching Whiskers, snuggled up on her sleeping bag, and petting him gently. His fur was so soft—and he was such a little cat, so different from Sandy.

As the movie went on, the other kittens padded back to the kitchen, looking for Snowball and their bed. But Whiskers curled up on top of Mia and fell fast asleep—and he was still there the next morning.

Chapter Six
The Very Shy Kitten

"Oh, Mia!" Dad laughed. "How did you get him to do that?" He'd just arrived to pick Mia up from the sleepover. Lisa and Anna had left already; they had to hurry off to dance class.

Mia shook her head very carefully.

"I didn't, Dad. He just climbed up there. I think he's eyeing my toast."

From his place on her shoulder,

Whiskers purred loudly, and Mia giggled as his long whiskers tickled her cheek. "I wish I didn't have to go home and say good-bye to you!"

Her dad exchanged a thoughtful glance with Emily's mom. "When will the kittens be ready to go to new homes?"

"Well, I was looking it up, and it seems that about 10 or 12 weeks old would be best. Ours are four weeks now, so they'll be 10 weeks old about halfway through December. So I thought around then. It's a little close to Christmas; that's the only problem. Everyone's so busy, and I don't want to be encouraging people to give kittens as presents."

"Why not?" Mia asked. She thought a

kitten would be a wonderful Christmas present. Emily was getting Satin for her birthday, after all.

"Well, people sometimes get a kitten for their children at Christmas, and don't really think about them growing up into big cats who need care. Then sometimes they're abandoned," Emily's mom added sadly. "Luckily, most kittens are born in the spring or summer. Snowball was a bit late!"

Mia reached up and tickled Whiskers under the chin. She could feel his purrs buzzing against her neck.

I could take you home, she thought to herself, just for a second. But then she remembered. She didn't want another cat—not after Sandy. Very gently, she reached up and lifted Whiskers off her shoulder, and took him over to the bed. "I'm sorry, sweetheart. I have to go."

Whiskers stared after her in surprise. Had Mia not liked him sitting on her shoulder? Why was she going? He wailed—a loud, sad kitten wail that made Mia flinch as she dashed into the hallway to grab her stuff.

She said good-bye to Emily quickly. She felt bad rushing off, but she just couldn't stay any longer. She was almost silent on the walk home, even though Dad kept trying to ask about the party.

"Mia, have you thought…?" Dad started, as they carried her things into the house. "Emily's mom talking about homes for the kittens made me wonder. You seem to get along so well with Whiskers."

He trailed off when Mia looked up at him with her eyes full of tears.

"I can't," she whispered. "I thought I could, but what about Sandy? I'm not going to forget him! I never, ever want another cat again!"

"You don't have to forget him, Mia…," Dad tried to say, but Mia raced off upstairs to her room and slammed the door behind her.

84

Over the next few weeks, Emily kept Mia updated as they started to look for new homes for the kittens. Her mom had put an ad in the newspaper, and the local shops that had bulletin boards. A couple of people had called about coming to see them already.

"Someone named Maria is coming over on Saturday to see them all," she told Mia as they ate their lunches. "I'm sort of half-excited, half-sad. I really want them all to have nice homes." Emily shook her head. "And at least we're keeping Satin."

Mia nodded. She wanted them to have good homes, too. Especially Whiskers. He needed a home with somebody who could love him properly, without always remembering another cat. Sandy was her forever cat. She couldn't replace him, not even with Whiskers.

Emily's mom showed Maria into the kitchen, where Emily and Leah were playing with the kittens.

"Oh, aren't they sweet! How many are there?" Maria asked, laughing as one of the tabbies sniffed her boots.

"Four, but we're keeping Satin—the black kitten. There are two female tabbies, and the little white boy. Did you want just one kitten?" Emily's mom asked. "We're thinking that the tabby girls might want to stay together— they're such a team."

"I was only planning on getting one," Maria said. "I can't see a white kitten...."

"He was here a minute ago!" Leah looked around the kitchen. "Now that they can climb out of their bed they're all over the place."

"He's a little shy," Emily's mom explained. "But he's very sweet once he gets used to you. Look, there he is!" She smiled, and pointed to the bed, where a little white head was poking out from under the fleece blanket. "I'll get him out." She picked him up and tried to pass him to Maria, but Whiskers squeaked in fright and hissed, his paws sticking out rigidly,

87

and his tail fluffed out to twice its usual size.

"Oh, dear. Don't make him if he doesn't want to," Maria said worriedly. "Poor thing. He really is nervous. There are a lot of cats where I live, and I'm not sure this little one would cope very well if he's so shy. I'm sorry— I'm sure you'll find homes for them all."

Emily's mom followed her to the door, and Emily and Leah looked down at Whiskers, who was now huddled in Leah's arms.

"Oh, Whiskers," Emily muttered.

"No one's going to want you if you do that every time. It's so silly! He wants to be Mia's kitten, I know he does."

Leah nodded. "I know. But we can't make her have him. Maybe she'll come around to the idea."

Emily sighed. "I wish she'd hurry up about it."

A couple of weeks later, Mia and her grandma stopped in at Emily's house on the way home from school, and found that only Whiskers and Satin were left.

"I'm not surprised Whiskers didn't like them. The two little boys were so noisy," Emily's mom was saying to

Grandma. "They thought Whiskers was adorable, and they were all set to choose him, but it was just like with Maria. They tried to cuddle him, and he actually shot out of the kitchen door, and went and hid in the closet under the stairs! So they decided they'd take the tabbies instead." She laughed. "And they're going to call them Molly and Polly. I don't think they'll ever be able to remember which is which!"

"So it's only Whiskers now?" Mia asked, as Emily's mom made Grandma some coffee. Mia sat petting the little ball of white fur curled up in her lap.

Emily nodded. "At least he still has Satin to play with. But Mom's decided that we're keeping only one. We have to find Whiskers a home, and no one wants an unfriendly kitten."

"He isn't!" Mia said indignantly. "He's a sweetheart. He's just shy." *But maybe that's a good thing*, she admitted to herself. *I really don't want him to go....*

Whiskers yawned, and wriggled himself comfortable again. Mia and Emily had been rolling balls of newspaper for Satin and him to chase, and he was exhausted. The kitchen was covered in shredded paper, though. He rolled over onto his back, all four paws in the air, showing off his fat, pinkish tummy. He was liking solid food more and more now, and after

91

he'd had a meal, he was practically circular.

"But he's so different with you...," Emily sighed. "He doesn't mind playing with me and Leah, and he'll let us pet him. But I don't think he's ever gone to sleep on me. And definitely not upside down! That means he really trusts you, you know."

Mia nodded. She didn't dare say anything, but she looked up at Grandma. She was smiling, and nodding as if she agreed with Emily. Maybe she was being silly. Was it like Grandma had said when the kittens were born—that she was still holding onto missing Sandy? Was she making herself sad on purpose? Maybe it was finally time to let Sandy go....

Chapter Seven
The Perfect Owner

"I'll come and get you at about six then, Mia," Grandma said one day after school. Grandma gave her a kiss, and Mia waved good-bye. Whiskers was already weaving himself happily around her ankles, purring. His purr had definitely gotten louder as he got bigger, Mia decided. He was 12 weeks old now, definitely old enough for a new home.

But no one seemed to want a shy, nervous little white cat. Mia didn't mind. She was looking forward to spending lots of time with Whiskers over Christmas vacation. It had even started to snow that morning, although the flakes hadn't really stuck to the ground. She was sure that Whiskers would look beautiful if they took him out to play in the snow. He would be invisible, except for his round blue eyes!

Whiskers patted at her leg with his paw, asking to be picked up. Mia came to see him almost every day now, but he still missed her when she wasn't there. One day maybe she would take him with her?

"Hello, Mister Whiskers." Mia picked him up and cuddled him.

"What should we do, hmm?"

"Homework!" Emily said, grinning and waving the sheet Mrs. Jones, their teacher, had given them for the project they had to do over Christmas vacation. It was the last week of the quarter, and neither of the girls really felt like working, but Mrs. Jones was the scariest teacher at their school. The project had to be planned, even if it was only a little more than a week until Christmas Day. "We have to figure out this project, remember? Come on. Bring Whiskers with you." She scooped up Satin, leaving Snowball alone in the hallway, looking quite relieved. Whiskers and Satin were so much bigger now, and so bouncy that they wore Snowball out.

"I can smell fish sticks," Mia said a while later. "So can Whiskers and Satin. Look at them!" The kittens were prowling up and down by Emily's bedroom door, their tails twitching eagerly.

"I think our plan sounds pretty good," Emily said, looking down at what they'd written. *'Animals in the Time of Queen Victoria.'* I'll bet no one else will have thought of that. It's a great idea, Mia."

Mia laughed. "I'll come up with the ideas, you do the writing. You almost finished the entire plan while I was cuddling Whiskers. Do you think our snack is ready? The smell of those fish sticks is making me hungry."

"Must be. Let's go and see." Emily opened the door, and the kittens shot out onto the landing and eyed the stairs uncertainly. They wanted to be down there with the delicious fishy smell—but they weren't really sure about stairs yet....

Whiskers looked at Mia pleadingly, and she laughed and picked him up. She carried him down to the kitchen, while Emily followed with Satin.

Emily's mom smiled as they came in. "Look at those kittens! I've never seen them look so hungry. We'd better find the fish-flavored kitten food."

"I think they'd rather have the fish sticks," Emily said, going to the cupboard for the can and spooning out the kitten food. "Ugh. This one smells the worst!"

But Satin and Whiskers raced to their bowls and gulped down the food eagerly.

Emily's mom had just passed Leah, Emily, and Mia their drinks when the phone rang. She went to answer it, fighting with her oven mitts. "Hello? Oh, yes…. That's right. There's actually only one kitten left now."

Mia smiled, pausing with her fork halfway to her mouth. A paw was patting her knee. Whiskers must have wolfed down his kitten food already, and now he was on the hunt for something even better. She scooped him up onto her lap, and fed him a tiny bit of fish stick. Emily's mom wasn't looking; she was concentrating on the phone call.

"Oh, you've been looking for a white kitten? That's wonderful. He's a little bit shy, though, that's the only thing. He's very friendly once he knows you, but he may not want to be picked up."

The person on the other end of the phone didn't seem to mind this. Emily's mom was nodding and smiling.

Whiskers stared up at Mia, hoping for some more fish stick. His whiskers shook with excitement as he reached up a little white paw to pat Mia's hand.

But she didn't give him any. She put down her fork, very slowly and quietly, and stared at him. The kitten's whiskers drooped. Mia's face had changed; she didn't look like the girl who'd been sneaking him scraps a moment before. She was pale and miserable. Whiskers meowed, his ears flattening against his head. What was wrong?

"Tomorrow evening? Yes, that would be great. See you then." Emily's mom put down the phone, smiling. "Someone wants to come and see Whiskers! Her name's Madeline, and she says she's adopted a nervous cat before, so she doesn't mind if he's shy. And she's always wanted to have a white kitten. It's perfect!"

Emily nodded, but she was looking worriedly at Mia.

Mia gulped. Whiskers was going to have a perfect home—and it wasn't with her. She'd let this happen. If only she'd been brave enough to say that she wanted him to be her kitten—that she still loved Sandy, but she'd said good-bye to him.

She stood up jerkily, cuddling Whiskers against her tummy, and passed him to Emily. "I'm sorry, I'm not feeling very well. I have to go home," she said, hurrying to the front door.

"Mia, wait! I'll call your grandma," Emily's mom said worriedly.

"It's okay, I'll be fine," Mia called back, tears already stinging her eyes as she wrestled with the front door lock. At last it gave, and she dashed down the sidewalk.

Meowing frantically, Whiskers made a flying leap off Emily's knee and chased after Mia. Where was she going? She hadn't even tickled his ears and scratched under his chin, like she usually did when she left.

He shot out of the front door, onto the path, and looked around. He'd never been out at the front of the house, only on carefully-guarded trips into the back yard. The yard was frozen over with a layer of frost, and snowflakes were flurrying down from the darkening sky. If Mia had been with him, Whiskers would have chased the strange fluffy things, but now he hardly noticed them. He had no idea where Mia had gone. He sat down on the path and wailed miserably for her.

But Mia couldn't hear him. She was almost home now, and she could hardly see through her tears, let alone hear a heartbroken kitten halfway up the road. She pressed the front doorbell over and over until Grandma came, looking worried.

"Oh, it's you, Mia! But I was coming to get you…. Mia, what's wrong?"

"Whiskers," Mia sobbed. "I was too late for Whiskers. I should have said

I loved him, and I didn't. How could I be so silly? You were right all along, Grandma, and now I've lost him!"

Grandma hugged her. "Oh, Mia. I'm so sorry. Has someone taken him?"

Mia nodded. "A lady's coming to see him tomorrow, and she's going to love him, I know she will."

"Tomorrow?" Grandma guided her inside and shut the door. "But Mia, why don't you go back to Emily and her mom and explain? Tell them you want him."

"But I can't!" Mia wailed. "I kept saying no, because of Sandy. They'll think I'm just going to change my mind again. And I told Dad that I never, ever wanted another cat. Dad and Mom would never let me have Whiskers now." She sat down on the bottom of the stairs with her chin in her hands. "Madeline—the lady who called—said she knows all about nervous cats, and she really wants him. Whiskers deserves to have an owner like that." She sniffed. "I should have been braver before."

Grandma sat down next to her. "I do see what you mean, Mia, but I think you're being too hard on yourself— and that poor little cat." She stared thoughtfully at the front door, and a small smile curved up at the corners of her mouth.

Mia didn't see it—she had her fingers pressed against her eyes now to stop herself from crying. She could see white speckles against her eyelids, and they reminded her of kitten fur.

"Are you sure?" Emily wrinkled her nose anxiously and glanced up, checking that Mrs. Jones hadn't seen them talking. "Won't it just make you feel worse?"

Mia shook her head. "No. I really want to say good-bye to him. I have to. I probably will feel horrible, but it would be awful to never see him again."

"I guess you're right." Emily sighed. "Madeline sounded really nice, from what Mom said."

"I know," Mia whispered. Then she shook her head, trying not to think about saying good-bye to Whiskers. "We're supposed to be writing about Victorian animals. Did you bring that book from the library?"

They got back to work—Mrs. Jones had said their project idea sounded excellent. But every time she stopped writing, Mia felt sad again, remembering Whiskers's soft white fur and those amazing whiskers! He was so different from Sandy, but he was special, too. The way he always wanted to climb all over her, and his clever trick of perching on her shoulder....

He'll be too big to do that soon, though, she thought. She'd never see what he looked like as a grown-up cat! Mia swallowed miserably.

She wasn't sure if the day raced by, or if it crawled. All their classes seemed to last forever, but soon it was time to go home. It seemed like all of a sudden, she was putting on her coat and grabbing her stuff, and following Emily to meet Leah outside the gates. And the walk home seemed to vanish in seconds. Mia felt almost sick as they went into Emily's house.

She expected Whiskers to bounce up to her purring as he usually did, but the house was very quiet. Snowball and Satin were curled up together in Snowball's old basket.

Mia swallowed. "Where's Whiskers?" she asked Emily's mom.

She looked around, hoping that he was hiding, and he was going to jump out and surprise her. But really, she knew that he wasn't. "He's gone, isn't he? That lady's already come by and taken him?"

Emily's mom was starting to say something, but Mia couldn't bear to listen. She was too late—even to say good-bye!

Emily rushed over and tried to give her a hug, but Mia gently pushed her away and ran home.

Grandma answered the door, looking excited, but Mia hardly saw her. She didn't even stop to listen to what Grandma was trying to say. She simply raced up the stairs to the safety of her bedroom, flinging herself onto her bed and hugging Sandy's old blanket.

Now she had lost both of them.

Chapter Eight
A Wonderful Surprise

Whiskers sniffed around the strange room worriedly. He didn't understand what was going on. He had been carried here in a box, and he hadn't liked it, his claws catching and scratching on the cardboard as he slid around, meowing and hissing. Then he'd been let out in this strange new place. He was sure he'd never been here before, but it smelled familiar somehow, and there was a bowl of his favorite food, and some water. The old lady had watched him, but she hadn't tried to pick him up. She'd just sat, very quietly, and every so often she whispered to him. He knew her. She came to visit with Mia sometimes—so why was she here, when Mia wasn't?

It was all very odd. He'd hoped that Mia might come and see him, after she disappeared so quickly the day before. But what if she didn't know where he was? He needed to get back home so Mia could find him.

The old lady had gone away now. She had hurried off when the doorbell rang. She'd closed the door behind her, Whiskers noticed, as he sniffed at it.

Or almost, anyway. The latch hadn't quite caught. Whiskers nosed it, and it swung open a little more. The curious kitten poked his whiskers around the door, and then his nose, and then the rest of him—and set off to search for Mia....

Whiskers pattered down the hallway, his nose twitching. He felt confused. Maybe Mia had come to find him after all. He was sure he could smell her. Or was he imagining it? He looked from side to side, wondering where to go. Food smells were coming from behind him, but from the noise it sounded like there were people upstairs. Stairs....

He trotted over and looked up the flight of stairs. They were very steep.

Luckily, they had carpet, or he would never have been able to get his claws in to struggle up. Whiskers scrambled up onto the first step, feeling proud of himself. He licked his paw and brushed it over his ears to settle his fur before he tackled the next step. And the next....

It took him a few minutes to heave and claw his way up to the top, and he rolled onto the last step, panting exhaustedly. His claws ached. But he was up! And he could hear voices coming from behind a door at the top of the stairs. His ears flattened. They were not good voices. Someone was upset. The second voice was the old lady who had been with him downstairs. She was doing that gentle, soothing talking again.

The door was open a crack, and he peered cautiously around it. The old lady was sitting on the bed, with a girl lying face-down beside her, patting her hair while she cried. Whiskers sniffed again. He'd never heard Mia sound like that before, but he was sure it was Mia. Would she be glad to see him? What was the matter with her? He hesitated by the door, uncertain what to do.

Then the old lady looked up and saw him. She looked surprised for a moment, but then she smiled and held out her hand to him, rubbing her fingers together, her face hopeful.

She wanted him to come closer.

"Mia, sweetheart, listen. I've got something to tell you. I'd have told you right away if it hadn't taken me so long to get up those stairs."

"I'm sorry, Grandma. I know you're not supposed to use the stairs. Oh, I should have told Emily's mom a long time ago that I wanted Whiskers to be ours...," a muffled voice sobbed.

That was his name. It was Mia— it had to be. She smelled right, and she'd said his name, even if her voice sounded all strange.

Whiskers bounded across the bedroom and looked up angrily at the bed. How was he supposed to get up there? The old lady stretched out her hand and scooped him up, smiling. "Mia...."

He had been right! Whiskers stumbled along the soft comforter until he was next to Mia's tangle of blond hair, standing on a blue fleece blanket. He nudged her with his nose, but she didn't notice, so he did it again, harder this time.

Mia raised her head. Her eyes were blurry and sore from crying, so for a moment she didn't understand.

Then Whiskers purred at her proudly. He had found her!

"Whiskers!" Mia gasped. "What are you doing here? Why aren't you at your new home? Did you run away? Emily's going to be so worried about you." She struggled to sit up, and gazed at the little white kitten sitting contentedly in the middle of her bed.

"That's what I was trying to tell you," Grandma said gently. "When you came home so upset last night, I had a talk with your mom and dad, and we all agreed. Your dad had been convinced that you should have Whiskers anyway. He wanted to bring him home a long time ago, but your mom was worried it would upset you again. So Dad and I went over to Emily's house and talked to her mom after you'd left for school this morning. We arranged for Whiskers to be your kitten. Well, and a little bit mine, for some company while you're at school. I know you shouldn't give animals as presents, but think of him as an early Christmas gift." Grandma smiled at her, a little anxiously. "Your mom was so upset that she had to be at work this afternoon. She wanted to see your face when you found out."

"But what about the lady who called? Madeline?" Mia asked. Her mind was spinning, trying to take all this in.

"Emily's mom called her to explain. She was very sympathetic, apparently.

She lost a cat recently, too; she said she knew how hard it could be."

"So Whiskers is really ours?" Mia looked down at the kitten, who was sniffing the cat blanket interestedly, his whiskers looking remarkably white against the navy blue fleece. She reached out and tickled him under the chin, with just one finger. She didn't dare do more. She felt like there was a dream kitten in her bedroom and if she touched him, he might disappear, like a bubble.

But he didn't. He purred loudly and gazed up at her with big blue eyes. He looked very, very pleased with himself.

"Yes, you are a clever little cat, finding your way up here," Grandma said, smiling. "I thought I'd closed him in my bedroom, Mia. I didn't want him wandering all over the house, feeling lost. But he obviously found a way out. He wanted to come and find you."

Mia nodded. "He's sitting on Sandy's blanket," she whispered suddenly, a strange sharp feeling clutching at her chest.

Grandma nodded. "Yes."

Mia took a deep breath. Whiskers nudged her knee with his nose and stood up, turning around a couple of times before settling himself into the perfect position, nose touching tail tip, like a little white fur cushion.

Mia let her breath out again, shakily. There were white hairs on the blanket now, mixed with the orange ones.

Whiskers opened one eye and yawned, showing a raspberry-pink tongue. Then he snuggled down further into the blanket and went to sleep.

Just like he belonged.

Mia yawned and rolled over, and felt Whiskers sigh in his sleep beside her. She'd had to move the fleece blanket now, to the side of her bed. Whiskers liked to sleep jammed between her and the wall, even though Mia sometimes worried that she would accidentally squash him.

She buried her head in her pillow and sighed happily. It didn't feel like time to get up yet. Then her eyes snapped open. It was Christmas Day!

"Whiskers! Look, my Christmas stocking." She sat up, and eyed the bulging red-and-white striped stocking happily. She could see a bag of her favorite candy sticking out of it. "And cat crunchies! Your favorite fish ones!"

Whiskers purred with pleasure. He didn't know why Mia wanted to wake up early, but he would do anything for fish crunchies. He patted happily at the ribbons as Mia unwrapped her stocking presents.

"It's almost seven o'clock," Mia said at last. "I wonder if Mom and Dad would mind being woken up yet? Or Grandma?"

She climbed out of bed and put on her robe, then padded out to the top of the stairs, with Whiskers following her.

124

She peeked through her mom and dad's bedroom door, but they were both still fast asleep. Dad had said last night that his best Christmas present would be to sleep in, so she scooped Whiskers up before he could go and leap onto the bed. He'd only been with them a week, but already he had a thing about Dad's feet. He liked to pounce on them, and Mia thought that probably wouldn't be Dad's ideal way to wake up.

She crept down the stairs. Grandma always woke up early; she said it was to do with being older than 70—she didn't need as much sleep anymore.

"I can hear you, Mia! Merry Christmas!" Grandma called, as Mia hesitated outside her door.

Mia slipped into Grandma's room.

"You're up already!" she said in surprise. Grandma was sitting in her armchair, with a magazine and a cup of tea.

"Yes, and I'm glad you're here. I've got a special present for you." Grandma reached over to her little table and picked up a flat, rectangular package, wrapped in shiny Christmas paper with a big bow. Grandma liked wrapping presents.

"'For Mia, with lots of love this Christmas—and for being brave,'" Mia read from the gift tag. "I don't understand."

"Open it, Mia. You'll see." Grandma nodded eagerly.

Mia put Whiskers down on the

floor, then started to undo the bow and peel off the paper.

"Oh, Grandma! It's beautiful!" It was a box, with a painting of a cat on the lid.

"But you haven't seen inside it yet. Open it up."

It wasn't actually a box, Mia realized, as she opened it. It was a hinged photo frame, made to hold two photos, one beside the other.

As though it was made for two very special cats.

Mia smiled, her eyes blurring a little with tears, but happy ones. On the left was Sandy, staring out at her, with his ears pricked up. *Grandma must have taken it just as he saw a butterfly to chase*, Mia thought. Sandy loved to hunt butterflies....

And on the right was a picture of her little Whiskers sitting on Grandma's windowsill. The winter sun was shining on his beautiful whiskers so that they sparkled.

"Thanks, Grandma. It's the most wonderful present." Mia hugged her, and laughed as there was a sudden rustling sound. Whiskers had jumped onto the discarded wrapping paper and was pouncing backward and forward, chasing an imaginary something. Maybe when he was bigger, Whiskers would chase butterflies, too....

The
Frightened
Kitten

Contents

For Lara

Chapter One
Packing to Move

"Please wrap it up carefully," Kate told Maddie, stuffing an armful of bubble wrap into her best friend's lap.

Maddie nodded, winding it around the picture frame. "Shadow looks handsome in this picture," she said, her voice a little shaky.

Kate nodded. "He always does. But that's my favorite picture of him."

Maddie stared down at the photo. She was in it, too. It had been taken last summer, and showed Kate and her, with Kate's huge black cat, Shadow, sitting on the rug between them. He was almost as tall as they were when the girls were sitting down.

Maddie laughed with surprise as a hard head butted her arm, and Shadow stomped his way on to her lap to see exactly what she was doing. He'd been asleep on the end of Kate's bed, but he'd obviously decided something interesting was happening. He was the world's nosiest cat.

"Do you think he'll mind moving?" Maddie asked, watching Kate fill a cardboard box with books and her trinkets, all carefully wrapped up.

"I don't know. " Kate shrugged. "The new house has a big yard, but he likes it here. Like me." She sighed miserably. "I keep hoping Dad's going to come home and say it was all a mistake, and he doesn't have to go and work in Chicago after all. But we're leaving tomorrow. It's getting a little late for that." She sniffed, and sat down next to Maddie and Shadow.

Maddie put an arm around her, and Shadow bounced onto Kate's lap, standing up on his hind legs to wrap his front paws around her neck. It was his trick. Kate always told people she had a cat who hugged, although he didn't do it to very many people. Mostly Kate, but he would do it to Maddie sometimes, especially if she'd given him a cat treat. He'd even done it to Maddie's dad once, when he came to pick Maddie up. Her dad had been surprised, but Maddie had noticed that he always looked for Shadow whenever he came to Kate's now. As though he was hoping that Shadow might do it again.

Maddie had been working on her mom and dad to let her get a cat of her own for a while. She was pretty sure that Shadow had won her dad over that day. Now she just had to persuade her mom....

Kate sniffed again. "What if he doesn't like the new house, Maddie? He might even try and find his way back here. You read in the papers about cats who do that."

"Chicago's probably too far for him to try it," Maddie said. It was meant to be comforting, but it didn't work. She didn't want to think about how far away her friend was going to be. And she was going to have to start a new school, of course. Maddie couldn't imagine having to do that.

Kate frowned. "I hope there aren't too many other cats near the new house.

Shadow's the top cat around here. None of the other cats would put a paw in our yard. But the new yard might be another cat's territory already."

Maddie looked down at Shadow, now sitting on Kate's lap. He yawned and stretched, and then stared up at her with huge green eyes. *He* didn't look like he was worried.

"Even if the yard is another cat's territory, I don't think it will be for long," Maddie said, petting him.

Kate nodded, laughing. "Maybe. He doesn't fight very often, but when he does, I think he just sits on the other cats and squashes them." She sighed. "I'd better finish packing. Mom says I should have had it finished yesterday." She pushed Shadow gently off her knee, and he slunk away to hide among the boxes.

Maddie went back to wrapping up the photo. She was going to miss Kate so much. She knew Kate would miss her, too, but her friend was a bit like Shadow, Maddie thought. She was so strong and confident. She'd have a new group of friends in no time, and she'd be showing off her famous hugging cat to them instead.

"Please pass me that tape, Maddie, so I can seal this box up."

Maddie handed her the packing tape, then wrapped another picture frame. "Where did Shadow go?" she asked, a few minutes later.

"He's under the bed, isn't he?" Kate said, peering down.

But he wasn't. There was a sudden thumping and then a muffled yowl. "He's in the box!" Maddie giggled.

Kate stared at the big cardboard box she'd just taped up. "He can't be...." she said, but she didn't sound very sure. She ripped off the tape, and the flaps came up, followed by a large black head, with angry, glowing green eyes. The cat scrambled out, hissing grumpily.

"Well, you shouldn't have been in there!" Kate laughed. "Nosy boy!"

Maddie was laughing, too. But even as she laughed, she was thinking, *I'm going to miss them so much....*

Kate and her mom walked Maddie home—it was a beautiful day, warm and sunny. Perfect Easter vacation weather. If Kate hadn't been leaving tomorrow, they'd have spent time in the park, or maybe gone out somewhere for the day.

"Those cats that live next door to you are nearly as big as Shadow," Kate's mom commented as they came up to Maddie's yard.

"They're sitting on Mom's daffodils again," Maddie sighed, as she tried to shoo the two big tabby cats off the stone pot that her mom had planted full of bulbs. For some reason, Tiger and Tom had decided it was a really good place to sit and take a nap, and the daffodils were looking a little squashed now.

Maddie's mom opened the front door. "I heard you coming, girls. Oh, no, not those awful cats again!"

Tiger spat angrily at Maddie as she got him off the daffodils. He was so different from sweet-natured Shadow. At last, he jumped down, and the two of them stalked away, glaring back at Maddie.

As the moms talked, Kate flung her arms around Maddie. "Promise you'll call me every day! Tell me everything that's happening at school, okay?"

Maddie nodded. "You're coming back to visit at Christmas break."

"We'd better go," Kate's mom said. "It'll be a long day tomorrow, and there's still some packing to do."

And that was it. Kate and her mom went back down the path, waving, and Maddie was left on her own.

"I'm finished," said Maddie, pushing away her half-eaten dinner. Mom had made her favorite pasta, but Maddie just wasn't hungry.

145

Her dad leaned over and put an arm around her shoulders. "Do you think we could tell her the news? To cheer her up?" he suggested to Maddie's mom, and she nodded.

"What news?" Maddie sniffed sadly.

"Do you remember I told you that my friend Donna's cat had kittens a couple of months ago?" Mom asked.

"Oh, yes. You showed me a picture. They're beautiful. There were some tortoiseshell ones—my favorite kind!"

"Good. Because one of them is going to be yours!"

Maddie blinked. "I'm getting a kitten?"

"You can choose which of the litter you'd like. Donna needs to find homes for them all, and we thought it would be nice for you to have a cat, since you've wanted one for so long. And especially since you're going to miss Kate. Getting to know a kitten might make things less sad." Her mom looked at her anxiously. "We're not trying to take your mind off of missing her, Maddie. It's a really sad thing for a friend to move away."

"It just seemed like a good time," her dad added.

Maddie nodded. "It *is* a good time," she whispered. She couldn't help feeling sad about Kate, of course, but at the same time, inside she was bubbling with excitement. *A kitten! A kitten! I'm getting a kitten!*

Chapter Two
The New Kitten

Maddie's mom showed her some more photos of the kittens. Three were tabbies and the other two were tortoiseshells, beautiful black, white, and orange cats. They were all snuggled around each other and their mother, who was black like Shadow. Maddie was pretty sure she would like a tortoiseshell—Tiger and Tom had turned her off from tabby cats.

"When can I see them?" Maddie asked the next morning at breakfast.

Mom smiled. "I've arranged for us to visit them today. And if you're sure which kitten you'd like, you can even bring it home! We can go to the pet store on the way to Donna's house to get everything we'll need."

As it turned out, they needed a lot of things. Maddie knew they would need a basket. And food and water bowls. But there was so much else. A collar. Grooming brush. Food. Special treats that were good for cleaning kitten teeth. Toys....

They were just about to go and pay for everything when Mom stopped. "Oh, I forgot that Donna said we needed to bring a cat carrier to take the kitten home."

Maddie smiled. *Home!* She loved the idea of their house being a home for a kitten.

"If you get anything else, we won't have room for the kitten in the car," Dad muttered, but Maddie knew he was only joking.

"Can we go to Donna's now?" she said hopefully, as they loaded all the things in the trunk a few minutes later.

Mom nodded, and hugged her. "I'm really excited."

Maddie threw her arms around her mom's neck. "I bet I'm more excited than you."

150

Dad got in the car and blew the horn at them. "Come on. I'm so excited I actually want to go and see these kittens sometime today!"

"Oh, look at them!" Maddie breathed, stopping in the kitchen doorway. The kittens were asleep in a large basket in the corner of the room. It was by the radiator, and the floor had been covered with newspaper.

"They're doing pretty well with their house-training; the newspaper's just in case they miss the litter box," Donna explained. "We've been keeping them in the kitchen up until now, but this past week they've been escaping!"

"How old are they?" Maddie asked. They looked so little. She couldn't believe they were ready to leave their mom.

"Ten weeks yesterday. I bought a book about raising kittens when we found out that Dilly was pregnant, and it recommended keeping them with their mom until then, so she can teach them what they need to know. Also, that way they get to spend more time with their brothers and sisters, and learn how to get along."

"So did you mean for her to have kittens then?" Maddie's dad asked.

Donna sighed. "No, it was a total surprise. We were planning to have Dilly spayed, but it was too late. As soon as she's recovered from having these, we'll take her to the vet. I love the kittens, but I don't want more!"

"Are you going to keep any of them?" Maddie asked, as she knelt down by the basket. "They're so beautiful."

Donna nodded. "I know. I'd love to keep a couple, and it will be sad for Dilly to lose them all, but we only ever meant to have one cat! We'll have to see. Many people seem interested in adopting one." She smiled at Maddie. "But you've got first choice. Your mom saved you a kitten weeks ago!"

Maddie looked up at her mom gratefully. "Thanks, Mom!"

"Well, it seemed like a perfect opportunity—you're old enough to help take care of a pet now."

"I'll be really good, I promise," Maddie said. "I'll even clean the litter box." She wouldn't mind, she thought, peering into the basket. The kittens had heard their voices, and were starting to wake up. Dilly was watching Maddie carefully, obviously guarding her babies.

One of the tabby kittens popped its head up and stared curiously at Maddie. She laughed, and his eyes widened in surprise.

"Oh, sorry!" Maddie whispered. "I didn't mean to scare you."

All the kittens were awake now, gazing at her with big green eyes. Maddie sighed. "How am I ever going to choose one of you?" she said. She didn't think she wanted a tabby kitten, but they were cute, too—their pink noses clashed with their orange fur.

One of the tortoiseshell kittens put its paws up on the side of the basket, and nosed at Maddie's hand. Its nose felt chilly and tickly, and Maddie stifled a laugh. She didn't want to make the kitten jump.

"Is this a girl kitten?" she whispered to Donna. She'd guessed that the tabby kittens were boys and the tortoiseshells were girls, but she knew it wasn't always the case.

"Yes. She's a sweetie. Very friendly. She loves to have her head petted."

The kitten looked at Maddie hopefully, and Maddie gently rubbed the top of her head. Maddie smiled. The kitten purred, and turned her head sideways, nestling into Maddie's hand.

"She's pretty," Mom said quietly.

"Can we take her?" Maddie breathed. The kitten was still purring and cuddling up against Maddie's hand. She was so little and perfect. Maddie was desperate to pick her up, but she wasn't sure she should.

The kitten solved the problem by clambering over the side of the basket—it was a soft, squashy one, and the sides were so high that she looked like she was trying to climb over a bouncy castle. There was a lot of scrambling, but eventually she landed on the floor, looking very proud of herself, and started climbing onto Maddie's lap.

"Oooh, claws." Maddie giggled, and gently put her hand under the kitten's bottom to help her up. The kitten finally reached Maddie's lap, looking worn out by the effort, but she purred delightedly when Maddie petted her fur.

"Well, it looks like she wants to be ours, too," Dad said, reaching out a finger to scratch behind the kitten's ears. "What are we going to name her?"

Maddie looked down at the kitten, who was busily curling herself into a neat little ball. "See that dark patch on her back? It's completely round. Don't you think it looks just like a cookie?"

"Cookie?" Mom laughed. "That's a really cute name for a cat. It does look like a little chocolate cookie against that white fur."

Maddie nodded. "It's the perfect name for her."

Maddie had the rest of the Easter vacation to get to know Cookie, and play with her. Her mom and dad were right—having her kitten did mean she spent less time worrying about going back to school without Kate. She also did a lot of reading—they'd bought a book on cat care at the pet store, and she took a couple more out of the library, too.

"Did Donna take the kittens to have their first vaccinations?" she asked Mom at breakfast, the day after they'd brought Cookie home.

Cookie was sitting on Maddie's lap, looking hopefully at Maddie's breakfast. The cereal looked just like her cat treats, she thought, but it didn't smell the same. She reached up, and sniffed harder. Definitely not cat treats, but a very good smell all the same. She put her front paws on the edge of the table, and darted her raspberry-pink tongue toward a drop of milk that Maddie had spilled.

It was sweet and cold, and Cookie gave a delighted little shiver. Maddie was looking at her cat book and didn't notice when Cookie edged forward, and stuck her tongue in the bowl to lap up the leftover cereal. She managed to get a few mouthfuls before Maddie spotted her.

"Cookie! You shouldn't be eating that! Oh, Mom, look! She has milk all over her whiskers!"

Cookie settled back on to Maddie's lap, licking her whiskers happily. She liked her food better, but it was nice to have a change....

"Oh, dear! I suppose a little bit won't do her any harm. You're done, aren't you? And yes, Donna gave us the vaccination certificate." Mom looked in the folder she'd left on the countertop. "She had them done about three weeks ago."

Maddie checked the book again. "Then we need to take her to the vet soon! She's supposed to have the second vaccination three weeks after the first one. And then in another three weeks, she'll be allowed to go outside."

"Actually, yes, that's what Donna's put in this note. She said we should probably have Cookie microchipped at the same time."

Maddie nodded. The tiny microchip went under the skin on the kitten's neck, and it would have a special number on it, so that Cookie could be easily identified by any vet if she got lost.

"I'll call the vet tomorrow," Mom said. "They're not open on Sunday."

Maddie nodded. "That reminds me! Can I call Kate, Mom? I have to tell her about Cookie!"

Luckily, the vet had a cancelled appointment on Monday afternoon. Maddie wanted to get Cookie's vaccinations done as soon as possible, so that she would be able to play with her in the yard. She knew that the little cat would love it. She was so adventurous inside the house. She kept climbing things, and she loved to tunnel under Maddie's comforter and then pop out at her.

163

For the trip to the vet, Maddie put the cat carrier next to her on the back seat, and Cookie peered out at her worriedly. She had only been in the cat carrier once, and that was to come to Maddie's house. Were they going back to her old home again? She did miss playing with her brothers and sisters, but Maddie was just as much fun to play with—and she didn't jump on her and try to chew her ears, like her big brother had done. Cookie definitely preferred Maddie's house. She let out a wail as Maddie lifted the carrier out of the car—but then she realized that it wasn't her old home they'd come to after all.

The place smelled very odd—sharp and chemical to her sensitive nose.

But at the same time, it was slightly familiar. Had she been here before?

Maddie put the carrier down on the floor, and Cookie sniffed suspiciously. There were other smells, too. A strange, worrying smell. It smelled like a dog. A dog had visited her old home once, and she hadn't liked it. She shifted nervously inside her carrier. It was coming closer!

Cookie gave a horrified squeak as a furry face loomed up in front of her carrier. The puppy peered in curiously and nudged the wire door with his nose.

The kitten bristled, her fur standing

165

on end and her tail fluffing up to twice its size. She hissed furiously at the dog. This was *her* carrier! She swiped her claws at his nose, but they scraped harmlessly down the wire.

"Barney, no!" his owner cried. "Oh, I'm so sorry. I hope he didn't scare your kitten."

Maddie's mom laughed. "Actually, I think she tried to fight back. She's a determined little thing."

Maddie looked anxiously into Cookie's carrier. "Are you all right? Sorry, Cookie, I was helping Mom fill out the forms. I didn't see what was happening." Then she smiled. Cookie was sitting in the carrier with her tail wrapped smugly around her. She wasn't afraid of some silly dog!

Chapter Three
Outdoor Adventure

"She's going to miss me while I'm at school," Maddie said worriedly. She had her coat and her backpack and her lunchbag—and a kitten sitting on her shoulder, sniffing with interest at the backpack. "It's the first day I won't get to play with her."

"I'll be here though," her mom replied. Maddie's mom worked

part-time at another school, but she didn't go in on Mondays or Fridays. "I'll play with her a lot, Maddie, I promise. And your dad's working from home tomorrow. Cookie will get used to being left alone. It'll be fine."

Maddie nodded doubtfully. She'd spent the entire vacation playing with Cookie and making a big deal about her. She just couldn't imagine a whole day at school without seeing her. And without Kate….

"Come on, Maddie. We'd better go."

Maddie sighed and then carefully unhooked Cookie's claws from her coat. She put her down gently and rubbed her ears. "Be good," she told her. "I'll be back soon."

Cookie stared up at her. She didn't

understand what was happening, but she could tell from Maddie's voice that she wasn't happy. The kitten gave an uncertain little meow and patted at Maddie's leg with a paw, asking to be picked up again.

"Maddie, now," her mom said firmly, seeing that Maddie was close to tears. She shooed her out of the door, leaving Cookie all alone in the house.

Cookie sat by the front door for a little while, hoping that they'd come back, but she couldn't hear any footsteps heading up the path. She didn't understand why Maddie left. Eventually, she padded back into the kitchen. She had seen Maddie and her mom and dad use the back door, even though she wasn't allowed out of it yet. Perhaps they would come in that way?

Cookie waited for what seemed like a very long time, but no one came in by that door, either. So she wandered through the house, meowing. Where had they all gone? Were they ever coming back? She looked at the stairs for a while, but she still found them very difficult to climb. Maddie had carried her up there a couple of times, but it took her a long time to get up the entire flight of stairs by herself.

Sadly, she trailed into the living room, and clawed her way up the purple blanket on the sofa. It already had quite a few claw marks on. Cookie had quickly discovered that the back of the sofa was an interesting place to sit. She sat down, peering out of the window, hoping to see Maddie coming up the front path.

Instead, she saw a large furry face staring back at her.

Cookie was so surprised that she jumped backward with a meow of fright, and fell onto the sofa.

What was that? Another cat? In her yard? Cookie had never been out in it, but she was sure that it was hers. She sat shivering on the sofa, not daring to climb up and look again. The other cat had been a lot bigger than she was. What if it was still there? At last, Cookie scrambled up the blanket again, and peeked over the back of the sofa.

The big tabby cat was gone.

Cookie was so relieved that she curled up on the back of the sofa and went to sleep.

"She was fine, Maddie!" Mom said, as they walked home from school. "When I got home from dropping you off and doing the shopping, she was asleep on the back of the sofa. And then the rest of the day I played with her every so often, and she was perfectly all right."

Maddie nodded, looking relieved. "I wonder if she was watching for us coming home, and that's why she was on the back of the sofa."

"Maybe." Her mom laughed. "Actually, I think she's just nosy. She likes watching people go past. Anyway, how was school?"

Maddie could tell that her mom was trying not to sound worried about her. She shrugged. "Okay."

173

"Who did you sit with?"

"Lucy. And Riley."

"And it was all right?"

Maddie didn't want to tell her mom that she'd felt miserable and lonely all day, and that even though Lucy and Riley had been nice, she'd hardly talked to them. She couldn't help thinking that they were Kate's friends, not hers, and they didn't really want to hang around with her. Luckily, there had been a kickball game at lunch, so she hadn't had to hang around on her own in the playground. But there wasn't a game every lunchtime. She sped up, hurrying home to see Cookie.

"Oh, look, she's there. Watching for us!" Maddie beamed. She ran up the path, watching Cookie leap off the back of the sofa. She could hear a little scuttle of paws, and then frantic meowing and a scratching noise as the kitten clawed at the door. As soon as her mom opened it, Maddie swept the kitten up to hug her.

School wasn't any easier the next day, or the day after that—but at least Maddie had Cookie to cheer her up at home. And she was really looking forward to Saturday—the vet had said Cookie could go out in the yard then, even though it wasn't quite three weeks since her shots. He'd said it would be fine as long as she wasn't around any other cats.

Maddie didn't give Cookie as much breakfast as usual on Saturday. And just in case Cookie did wander too far, Maddie made sure she had a full bag of the kitten's favorite chicken treats.

Cookie was still staring suspiciously at her food bowl, wondering why breakfast hadn't seemed to take as long to gobble down as usual, when she realized that the back door was wide open. She'd seen it open before, of course, but only when someone was holding her tightly, and even then it always slammed shut before she could wriggle free and go investigating. She crept over to it, keeping low to the ground, expecting any minute that Maddie or her mom would catch her.

But Maddie was outside! She was standing by the door, calling her! Cookie hurried so fast out the door that she almost tripped over the step. She shook herself angrily and pattered down the path to where Maddie was.

There were so many smells! She sniffed curiously at the grass, and patted it with one paw. It was cool and damp, and taller than she was!

"Do you have the treats?" Her mom appeared in the doorway. "In case Cookie goes running off. Remember, she could get under the fence if she really tried."

Maddie waved the foil packet. "It's okay. Oh, look! She saw a butterfly!"

The orange butterfly was swooping carelessly past Cookie's nose, and the kitten watched it in amazement. Maddie had dangled pieces of string for her, and feathery toys, but she had never seen anything like this. She reached out her paw and tried to bat at the butterfly, but it flew behind her, and she almost fell over trying to chase after it.

"You can't have it, Cookie," Maddie laughed. "I don't think butterflies are

very good for you. And they're all legs
and wings; I bet they don't taste good."

Cookie stared after the butterfly,
which was flittering over the fence to
the yard next door. She thought
it looked delicious. But there
was no way she could get
over the high fence to
follow it.

Chapter Four
Tiger and Tom

Maddie and Cookie spent so much time playing in the yard that on Friday evening, Maddie's dad came home with a surprise. He put the big box he was carrying down in front of Cookie's cat basket.

"What is it?" Maddie asked, looking at the front of the box. Cookie blinked at it sleepily. She was worn out from running around the yard with Maddie after Maddie had gotten home from school.

"Oh, a cat flap! Thanks, Dad!"

"We can put it in tomorrow. It's been more than three weeks since Cookie had her vaccinations now, so we can let her out on her own."

Maddie nodded. "I guess so. But she's not even 14 weeks old. She's still so little."

"I think cats like to explore, though," Dad pointed out. "She'll be able to climb trees. Chase more butterflies...."

Cookie suddenly perked up, bouncing up and staring at him, ears pricked. Dad laughed. "You see?"

Maddie had been worried that Cookie might not be able to open the cat flap, or that she just might not like it—Kate had told her that it had taken Shadow a while to get used to his. But as soon as Cookie understood what the cat flap did, she took to it immediately. She spent most of Saturday afternoon popping in and out of it, coming back into the kitchen every five minutes to make sure that Maddie was still there.

Maddie had been nervous that Cookie might try leaving the yard. But even though Cookie had sniffed at the holes under the fence, there was plenty in Maddie's yard to keep her busy.

Maddie was doing her homework on Sunday morning, with Cookie curled on her lap. Her science worksheet seemed to be taking forever. It was probably because she kept thinking about her science class on Friday. She'd had to pair up with Sara, a girl she didn't really like, and Sara had kept on making mean little comments during class. So now every time she tried to write about the differences between solids and liquids, she just started thinking about how much she missed having Kate to work with. Kate would have said something funny about Sara, Maddie was sure.

At least Maddie saw that Becky, one of the girls who sat at the table behind Maddie, had rolled her eyes at Maddie in an "Ignore her!" sort of way, and Maddie had smiled back.

Now Cookie yawned and jumped off Maddie's lap, heading for her cat flap. She was bored with sitting still, and Maddie didn't seem to want to play. Cookie had chased some colored pencils across the table, but Maddie had put them away instead of rolling the pencils for her to chase.

The yard was full of interesting smells, and some bees were buzzing around the lavender bushes. Cookie watched them, fascinated, her tail tip twitching. She was watching so closely that she didn't see Tiger and Tom sneaking under the fence next door. It wasn't until the two big cats were right behind her that Cookie heard them creeping through the grass, and whirled around. She was sure it was one of these cats who'd been staring in at her through the window.

The tabby cats had their ears laid back as they snuck toward her. Cookie backed away from them into the lavender bush. She knew the two cats weren't friendly. Her tail bushed out, and she threw a nervous glance toward the door. Could she make a run for her cat flap? But one of the bigger tabby cats, the one with the torn ear, was between her and the house, his tail swishing from side to side.

Tiger, the one with the darker stripes, was almost nose to nose with her now, hissing and staring. Cookie was squashed into the lavender bush— she couldn't go back any further.

Tiger slapped her on the head with one enormous paw, sending her rolling, and Cookie wailed miserably. What was she supposed to do? Why were they attacking her?

Inside the house, Maddie was still gloomily eyeing her homework. She glanced up as her mom came into the kitchen, looking confused.

"Maddie, can you hear a strange noise? It almost sounds like a baby crying. A sort of howling."

Maddie yelped and suddenly pushed her chair away from the kitchen table, racing as fast as she could for the back door. She was sure it was Cookie.

She flung open the door, and Tom jumped, hissing at her, but Tiger and Cookie hardly seemed to notice. They were in the middle of the lawn now, and Tiger was about three times the size of Cookie with all his fur fluffed up. They were making all kinds of strange noises still, circling around

187

each other. As Maddie watched, Tiger leaped on Cookie again, and the two cats seemed to roll over and over, twisting and scratching.

"Stop it!" Maddie yelled. She raced over to them, shoving Tiger, ignoring the hissing and scratching at her hands. She snatched Cookie up, and yelled at Tiger and Tom, sending them scurrying away under the fence.

"Maddie, are you all right?" Her mom came running out. "It all happened so quickly. I didn't realize what was going on. Is Cookie hurt?"

"I don't think so, but she's shaking." Maddie carried the kitten inside. "Those horrible cats!"

Her mom sighed. "I suppose they're used to coming into our yard. They think Cookie's in their territory."

"Well, she isn't!" Maddie snapped. "It's our yard and our cat!"

"Yes, we know that, but I bet the cats don't. Give her to me. You need to wash your hands. They must hurt. You're all scratched!"

Reluctantly, Maddie handed Cookie over to her mom.

"She's so scared," Maddie said, her

voice shaking. "Tiger's so much bigger than Cookie. He could have really hurt her." Then she laughed a little. "I saw Cookie scratch his nose, though, before he ran off."

"Did they go under the fence?" her mom asked. "Is there a hole we could block up?"

Maddie dried her scratched hands. "I'll go and see."

Cookie gave a worried little meow as she saw Maddie open the door, and Maddie stopped to pet her. "Don't worry. I'm not going to let those big cats anywhere near you."

She hurried out into the yard, checking the fence. There were holes all the way down the fence—big enough for a cat to squeeze through. It was going to be difficult to block them all up. And the fence wasn't that high, either. She was pretty sure that Tiger and Tom could climb it without too much effort.

"What are you doing?" someone asked in a snippy sort of voice.

Maddie stood up next to the flower bed. It was her neighbor, Josh, who owned Tiger and Tom. He was a couple of years older than she was and went to high school, so usually Maddie was too shy to say much to him. But not today.

"I'm looking at the fence! Your cats just came into my yard and attacked my kitten!" she snapped at him.

Josh shrugged. "Sorry. But cats fight. It's what they do."

"Don't you care? She's terrified!"

"There's nothing I can do. Cats chase each other and they fight. There are a lot of cats around here. Your kitten's going to get into fights, Maddie. Stop being such a girl."

"OH!" Maddie huffed, and she stomped back inside. Cookie was not going to fight, because Maddie wasn't going to let any other cats hurt her. Maddie didn't care how scratched *she* got.

But as she shut the kitchen door, slamming it hard enough to set the cat flap swinging, Maddie had a sudden, awful thought.

She could protect Cookie now, but what about tomorrow, when she went back to school?

"Maybe we shouldn't have gotten a cat flap," Maddie said worriedly.

Her dad scratched his head thoughtfully. He hadn't been home when Cookie got into the fight, and had missed the whole thing. "I can't exactly put that chunk of door back.

Anyway, Cookie's getting bigger all the time. She won't be such an easy target for those cats next door soon."

"I don't think Cookie's ever going to be as big as they are," Maddie said. "But it's good for her to be able to go out. She loves being in the yard! Or she did, anyway," she added sadly.

Cookie hadn't been outside again since the fight that morning. She'd retreated into the dining room. There was a nice patch of warm sun coming through the glass doors at the back of the room. Cookie lay in it, feeling the soft warmth on her fur. It made her feel better—not so jumpy and scared.

She stretched out on the carpet lazily and gazed out of the big window through half-open eyes, hoping to see some butterflies.

Instead, the next time she blinked, Tiger and Tom were there. In her yard, staring at her, just on the other side of the window.

Cookie's tail fluffed up, and she hissed in panic. For a moment, she forgot that there was glass there and they couldn't reach her through it. She was sure that Tiger was about to knock her over again. She raced out to the kitchen and Maddie, meowing in fright.

"They're back!" Maddie picked Cookie up, cuddling her.

Dad quickly filled up a glass that was by the sink and headed out into the yard. But he came back shaking his

195

head. "I was going to splash them—cats don't like getting wet—but they were gone already."

"If they keep doing this, Cookie's going to be frightened all the time," Maddie said anxiously. "It's so unfair."

She was still worrying when she went to bed that night. She'd left the kitten snoozing in her basket in the kitchen, after putting some of Cookie's favorite cat treats in her bowl, in case she woke up needing a midnight snack.

It took Maddie a long time to get to sleep. She tossed and turned, thinking about Tiger and Tom, and then about school tomorrow. Somehow her thoughts all got mixed together so that she was sitting in math class with Tiger and Tom (in the school uniform) on either side of her. Tiger was just telling her that she'd gotten her multiplication wrong, when Tom started howling in her ear. Maddie twitched, turned over—and woke up. That awful noise wasn't in her dream—the sound was coming from downstairs!

She flung herself out of bed and dashed down the stairs. The noise was louder now, and it was coming from the kitchen. Maddie couldn't understand—it sounded like more than one cat, but only Cookie was supposed to be in there. She shoved open the door, and saw Tiger and Tom by Cookie's food bowl, gobbling down the cat treats that she'd left out.

"Go away!" Maddie yelled. "Out! Bad cats!" Tiger and Tom hissed at her, but hightailed it out of the cat flap. The cat flap—of course. That's how they'd got into Maddie's kitchen!

"What on earth...?" Dad appeared in the kitchen doorway, looking sleepy.

"The cats from next door came in through the cat flap, Dad; they were eating Cookie's food!" Maddie crouched down by Cookie's bed. The kitten looked terrified, and as Maddie gently picked her up, she could feel how tense Cookie was, ready to leap out of Maddie's arms and run away at any moment. Her whiskers were twitching, and her little eyes were huge.

Mom had been worried that Cookie might end up making a mess in Maddie's room if she slept upstairs, but Maddie couldn't bear the thought of leaving Cookie on her own.

"Dad, please can I take Cookie upstairs to sleep with me?" she begged. "I know Mom said she should stay in the kitchen, but she's so scared."

Dad sighed. "Well, she is house-trained now. And she's pretty good on the stairs, too. She'll be okay to come down if she needs her litter box. I'm going to put a chair in front of the cat flap in case Tiger and Tom come back."

Maddie nodded. Cookie was relaxing a little now, but she was still looking around nervously. Maddie hurried upstairs and fluffed up her comforter into a cozy kitten nest at the end of the bed. It didn't leave much comforter for her, but she didn't mind.

Cookie stepped into the warm nest and padded at it with her paws. Maddie was here. She was safe. Tiger and Tom wouldn't be able to come upstairs. And if they did, Maddie would chase them away.

Maddie slipped into bed. She'd wanted Cookie to sleep on her bed since she'd gotten the kitten, but she wished it hadn't happened like this.

Maddie was just falling asleep again when she felt little paws padding up her tummy, and a soft wisp of fur brushed across her cheek as Cookie curled up on the pillow. Maddie giggled. Cookie's tail was lying on Maddie's neck and it tickled.

"We'll figure out what to do," she told Cookie sleepily. "It'll be okay."

Chapter Five
A Good Hiding Place

"Time to get up!" Maddie's mom pulled open the bedroom curtains.

"Mmmm. Oh!" Maddie suddenly remembered that Cookie was upstairs with her, although Cookie wasn't asleep on her pillow anymore.

"Dad told me he'd let you bring Cookie up here. I guess it's fine, as long as you make sure she doesn't get shut in. We don't want her peeing on your bedroom carpet!" She looked around. "Where is she? Did she go downstairs already?"

Maddie sat up quickly. "She was sleeping next to me."

"She's here!" Her mom was crouching down, peering under the bed. "It's all right, Cookie. I'm not scary. Oh dear, Maddie; she looks very nervous."

"Maybe she heard you coming in and thought it was Tiger and Tom again." Maddie hopped out of bed to look underneath.

Cookie was squeezed as far back as she could go, pressed against the wall. Maddie saw her whiskers trembling. "Cookie! Come on, it's okay."

Slowly, Cookie crept out. Maddie picked her up, but she flinched when Maddie's mom tried to pet her.

"She's usually so friendly," Maddie's mom said sadly. "Maybe she'll feel better after some food."

"I hope so." Maddie carried Cookie downstairs with her once she'd gotten dressed. She could feel Cookie tensing up as they came down the hall into the kitchen. She was practically clinging on to Maddie's sweater, and she didn't seem very interested in eating even when Maddie filled up her bowl.

"Don't worry. I'll keep an eye on her while you're at school," Mom said. "How are things going, anyway?"

Maddie shrugged.

"I know you miss Kate, but I'm sure there are lots of other people in your class that you could talk to," her mom said persuasively.

But none of them is as nice as Kate, Maddie thought. *And no one wants to talk to me. It's just not that easy....*

"It's a month until Field Day," said Mrs. Melling, Maddie's teacher, as she led everyone out on to the school field. "So we're going to practice long-distance running, relay races, hurdles, that sort of thing."

Several people sighed grumpily, but Maddie smiled. She loved to run. And she was pretty good at it, too. She'd been worrying about Cookie all morning, even though Dad had blocked the cat flap in case Tiger and Tom tried to get in again. Maddie knew Cookie should be just fine, but she couldn't stop thinking about Cookie, and how frightened she'd been. Maddie hoped that some running in the warm sun would shake off the jittery, miserable feeling inside her.

The field had an oval track painted on to the grass, and after they warmed up, Mrs. Melling divided them into groups to run heats. Maddie won her first heat easily—none of the others was really trying—but she was surprised when she beat a couple of boys in the next race. Some of the girls even started cheering for her at the end.

"Great job! You're so quick!" Becky came over and patted her on the back.

Maddie laughed nervously. She'd always liked Becky, but Becky was popular and had lots of friends. She was nice to Maddie, but they'd never hung around together much.

"Beat Joe in this last race, please!" Becky begged. "He's so full of himself. Look at him!"

Joe was talking to the other boys and doing show-off stretches. He obviously thought he was going to win.

"Okay." Maddie grinned. She wasn't tired at all. As they lined up for the last race, she bounced on her toes, staring at the finish line. As soon as Mrs. Melling blew her whistle, Maddie shot away, sprinting as fast as she could, and crossed the finish line just ahead of Joe.

"Yay! Maddie won!" She could hear Becky yelling above all the others. It felt fantastic.

With Becky and the others hugging her and telling her she was a star, it was easy to laugh off Joe growling about girls always cheating. And Becky's table in class was behind hers, so Maddie could see Becky grinning at her every so often as they had reading after PE. It was the best time she'd had in school all quarter. She couldn't wait to tell her mom and dad about it. They kept asking how school was going, and it would be nice to be able to say she'd had a fun day.

"How was Cookie?" Maddie asked hopefully, as she rushed up to her mom after school.

Mom made a face. "She's been scratching the sofa! I had to keep her out of the living room."

"Oh…." Maddie frowned. Cookie had never done that before. She hoped mom wasn't too angry.

When they got home, Maddie put her bags down, expecting the kitten to bounce up to her, wanting to play, like she usually did. But Cookie didn't come running.

"Cookie!" Maddie looked around anxiously.

"Try upstairs," her mom suggested. "She seems to like it there now."

Maddie ran up to her room. She couldn't see Cookie, but she had a horrible feeling she knew where the kitten was. Maddie knelt down, looking under the bed. She was right. Cookie was curled up in the corner again, looking at her with wide, worried eyes.

"Oh, Cookie," Maddie whispered. "It's all right, sweetie, come on out."

"I don't think we can keep the cat flap blocked," Dad said, looking down at his ice cream thoughtfully. "Cookie needs to be able to go out."

"But she doesn't want to," Maddie explained. "She's scared."

"It isn't good to keep her in. She should be sharpening her claws on trees, not the sofa," Mom sighed.

211

"And it would be nice not to have to keep cleaning out the litter box!"

"I'll do it," Maddie said quickly. "I don't mind. She's too scared to go in the yard."

She licked ice cream off her spoon, but she wasn't really hungry anymore. She could feel Mom and Dad both looking at her. And she was pretty sure they thought she was worrying too much.

"I think Cookie might just need to toughen up a bit," Dad said gently.

"She's definitely getting bigger," Mom pointed out. "She'll be as big as Tiger and Tom soon."

"I bet she won't," Maddie said. "And however big she is, there's still only one of her. Tiger and Tom work as a team, Mom! Like wrestlers!"

Her mom frowned and glanced meaningfully at her dad. Maddie knew what that look meant. They thought she was upset about Cookie because of school. Because she was feeling nervous and worried, too. Mom and Dad reckoned Maddie needed to make some new friends.

"I'll see if I can find some ideas," she said quickly, wanting to get away before they started asking about school again, and if there was anyone she wanted to invite over to play. *Maybe I could ask Becky over*, she thought, and then crushed the idea firmly. Becky was much too popular to want to hang around with her.

"You want to do what?" Josh made a snorting noise.

"Take turns," Maddie repeated, wriggling to keep her elbows on top of the fence. She was standing on a bucket to see over the fence, and it was a bit wobbly. "You keep Tiger and Tom in some of the time, so Cookie can go out without them scaring her."

After a snack, she'd searched her favorite pet advice websites, and found an email waiting for her from Kate. Maddie had sent her a message a couple of days ago, asking if she had any advice. The turn-taking idea was something Kate had read about once, and it sounded perfect.

Maddie took a deep breath. She didn't like talking to Josh; he always made her feel silly. But she had to. "Please can you think about it? Cookie is getting really twitchy and nervous. It wouldn't have to be long. Maybe only for an hour a day? Just until she's bigger and can stand up for herself."

Josh shrugged. "How am I supposed to keep them in? Tiger and Tom have a cat flap. They go in and out whenever they want to."

"But couldn't you—" Maddie began.

"I've got football. I need to go," Josh interrupted. And he disappeared through his back door, leaving Maddie peering after him.

Maddie sighed. Taking turns had seemed like such a good idea. Except that Josh couldn't be bothered!

She trailed back into the kitchen and found Cookie sitting on one of the chairs, staring anxiously at the cat flap—Maddie had moved the chair blocking it so she could get out.

"We'll have to think of something else," she told Cookie, tickling her under the chin.

Cookie rubbed her head against Maddie's hand and purred.

She really trusts me, Maddie thought. *I have to figure this out.*

Chapter Six
Cookie Gets Lost

Cookie didn't go out on her own at all for the rest of the week. Maddie took her out into the yard a few times, since she was pretty sure Tiger and Tom wouldn't come into the yard if Maddie was there. But as soon as she put Cookie down, the kitten would race for her cat flap. And even when she was inside, she spent most of her time hiding under Maddie's bed. She even peed on the floor, which made Mom angry.

"I know it isn't her fault, Maddie," mom told her as she scrubbed the carpet. "But the smell is horrible!"

"You don't want us to give her back to Donna, do you?" Maddie asked anxiously.

Mom shook her head. "No. But we need to figure this out. Anyway, we'd better get going to school now."

Cookie watched them from under the bathroom towel rack. She liked it there. It was warm and dark, and the bathroom didn't have any windows to see other cats. She hadn't gone downstairs to eat yet. She just wasn't sure she was brave enough. What if

Tiger and Tom came back into the kitchen again?

As the front door banged behind Maddie, Cookie crept to the top of the stairs. She was so hungry that she would have to risk going to the kitchen. She hurried down the stairs and peered around the kitchen door. No sign of any strange cats. Gratefully, she hurried in and started to gulp down her food, stopping every few seconds to glance around worriedly.

When she had eaten about half of her food, she began to relax a little to enjoy the meal.

Then the front door banged and she leaped away from the bowl in fright. Was it Tiger and Tom again?

Panicking, Cookie shot into the corner of the kitchen, trying to hide. She was so scared that she peed all over the floor.

"Oh, no! Cookie!" Maddie's mom said angrily, as she got back and saw the mess. "What on earth did you do that for? It's only me." She went to the cupboard under the sink to get some spray and a cloth. "Go on, shoo. I've got to clean this up." She flapped the cloth at Cookie grumpily.

Cookie was so jittery that the flash of white cloth scared her, and she shot out of the cat flap to get away from it. Maddie's mom had gone to get the mop, and she didn't notice that the kitten was gone.

Cookie sat on the back step, staring

around the yard. She hadn't been outside for a week, and there were so many tempting smells. And there were bees buzzing near the lavender bushes. And butterflies…. She padded out on to the lawn, feeling the warmth as the sun hit her fur.

She didn't even see Tiger before he leaped out from under the fence and spat at her. She turned to race for the cat flap, but he chased her, knocking her sideways and clawing her ear. Cookie looked around for Tom, wondering if he was about to jump out at her, too, but Tiger was on his own for once. Not that it mattered at all—he was still more than twice as big as she was and horribly fierce. Cookie meowed as Tiger pounced at her again.

She was never going to be able to get away. Unless…. She tried to scratch him, shooting out a sharp-clawed paw, and he retreated a little, hissing. It gave her time to think.

If she couldn't beat him running, maybe she could go over the fence? It was worth a try. She jumped at Tiger, clawing him again, and then raced past him, heading for the fence. She raced up it, scrambling and fighting for the top. Then she perched there, wobbling, and looked down at Tiger, who stared back up at her.

Cookie gave a frightened little squeak, then jumped off the other side of the fence....

"Mom, where's Cookie? I thought she'd be under my bed, but I can't find her anywhere. I've looked in all the places she usually goes."

Mom frowned. "I haven't actually seen her much today. She peed on the kitchen floor this morning. But I'm not sure when I saw her after that. I had to go shopping, and then I came straight back from the store to pick you up."

Maddie looked at Cookie's bed, as if she might suddenly appear from underneath it. Then she noticed the cat flap. "Oh! You moved the chair!"

"I had to," Mom said grimly. "I was wiping up cat pee around it. I see what you mean, though. She might have gone out. But that's good, Maddie! We want her to go outside again."

"Not if those two cats are around," Maddie muttered. "I'm going to check outside for her."

But there was no sign of Cookie in the yard either, even after Maddie called and called.

"Did you find her?" her mom asked, leaning out the kitchen door. She was looking slightly worried now, too.

224

"No, and we usually feed her right about now."

"I'll look upstairs again. Maybe she got shut in somewhere," Mom said.

Maddie had already checked everywhere, but she nodded anyway. "Cookie! Cookie!" she called again.

"Did you lose your kitten?"

Maddie jumped. She hadn't realized Josh was out in his yard. "Yes. You haven't seen her, have you?"

"Nope."

"Could you watch for her? Please?" Maddie asked.

"Yeah, all right." But he didn't sound very convincing, Maddie thought.

She ran back inside. "Mom, do you think we should go and look for her? Oh, but we can't!"

"Why not?" Her mom looked confused.

"If your cat gets lost, it's best to leave someone familiar in the house—otherwise, the cat might not think it's the right home if it comes back. My book said so."

"Really? Okay, well, if she's not back when Dad gets home, you and I can go and look for her then."

The hour before Maddie's dad got home seemed to drag. Maddie kept searching the same places over and over, just in case she'd somehow missed Cookie all the times she'd checked earlier.

As soon as she saw her dad at the gate, Maddie was out of the front door and running down the path.

"Cookie's lost! We're going to look for her! Stay here!" she gasped.

Her dad stared at her, and then at Mom.

Maddie's mom looked at him worriedly. "I said we'll go and look around the streets. I don't think she could have gone far."

Maddie was already hurrying along, looking under parked cars. "Come on, Mom!" she called.

Cookie peered miserably out at the strange yard. She'd jumped off the fence, and trying to look behind her at the same time, she'd landed badly, injuring one of her front paws.

227

It hurt, and so did the scratches. But she'd kept going, desperate to get as far away from Tiger as she could. She'd crawled under fence after fence, hurrying on and on, until at last she felt as if she might be safe. She'd smelled several other cats and even seen a couple, but none of them had chased her yet.

Eventually she'd stopped to rest behind a yard shed. She didn't feel like she could go any further; her paw hurt so much. She'd huddled there for the rest of the day, unsure what to do. She couldn't go home, could she? Tiger would chase her again. She'd have to wait until she was sure Maddie was back; then it would be safe.

They searched for a long time. Maddie kept looking at the road and hoping that Cookie hadn't run out in front of a car. *I should have taken better care of her. I should have made Josh do something about Tiger and Tom*, she kept thinking. *When I find Cookie, I'm going to tell him!*

They were halfway down the next road and Maddie was hanging over a wall, staring into some tall flowers, when a surprised voice said, "What are you doing?"

Maddie jumped. She hadn't even

noticed anyone approaching. Becky from school was standing behind her, while her mom locked up the car. She was wearing a cardigan over ballet clothes, and peering over the wall to see what Maddie was looking at.

"Hi, Becky. I'm looking for my kitten." Maddie swallowed. "She's lost…." It was so horrible to say it.

"Oh, no! The cute little tortoiseshell one? You've got her picture in your locker, don't you?"

Maddie nodded. She was surprised Becky had noticed.

"Want me to help look? Can I, Mom? We were just coming back from ballet," Becky explained. "This is our house. I didn't know you lived so close to us."

Maddie blushed. "Sorry about looking in your yard," she said to Becky's mom.

"Don't worry," Becky's mom replied with a smile. "You can help Maddie look, Becky. But only until it's dark—you've probably got another half an hour, that's all."

Maddie looked around anxiously. Cookie had never even been out at night! She hated the thought of her being all alone in the dark.

The two girls went on up the road, calling for Cookie, and Becky's mom joined in, too, asking their neighbors if they'd seen a kitten. But no one had.

"We have to stop. It's too dark," Maddie's mom said eventually.

"We can't!" Maddie said pleadingly.

"I'll come and help you look first thing tomorrow," Becky told her, giving her a hug. "Don't worry. We'll find her."

As it was starting to get dark, Cookie decided she could leave her hiding place. Maddie must be home by now. As long as Cookie could get back in through her cat flap before Tiger spotted her, she would be safe.

She crawled out of the dark space behind the shed, wincing as she tried to put her weight on the hurt paw. It seemed to be getting worse. She limped across the yard, and squeezed under the fence, only to see a pair of glinting amber eyes, glaring at her from under a bush. She backed away nervously. Her first thought was that it was Tiger, but it didn't smell like him. It was a strange smell—strong and fierce. And the creature it belonged to was big....

The fox darted forward and snapped at her, his teeth huge and yellow.

Cookie ran blindly. She didn't know

where she was going—just away. She darted down a side path, under a gate and out on to the pavement, where she stopped and glanced quickly behind her. The fox wasn't following. But now she had even less of an idea where she was, and her paw was throbbing after her panicked dash. She limped on, hobbling down the curb. She needed to rest, and there was a yard on the other side of the road that looked like a good hiding place, overgrown, with bushes spilling over a low fence. Cookie set off across the road, not seeing the car turning the corner.

She was halfway across when she noticed it—the huge machine that seemed to be towering over her, its lights dazzling her. The car braked sharply, its tires squealing on the road. Cookie wailed as she dived forward out of the way, her injured paw collapsing underneath her, so that she half-dragged herself across the road. She struggled through the gate of the overgrown yard and flung herself down under the dark bushes, her breath coming in terrified gasps. She was so tired, and everything seemed to hurt.

Cookie lay there, gazing into the dark night. She had no idea where she was, or how to get back to Maddie. What was she going to do?

Chapter Seven
Reunited!

Becky's mom dropped her off first thing on Saturday morning. "It's not too early, is it?" Becky asked. "Mom said it might be, but I told her you'd want to get looking right away."

Maddie half-smiled. "I've been up for a while. I'm just waiting for Dad. It's really nice of you to come."

Becky shook her head. "I said

I would! I want to help you find her."

Maddie's dad appeared behind her. "Ready, girls?"

As they came out of the gate, Tiger and Tom prowled down Josh's front path and leaped onto the wall, staring at them with round green eyes.

Maddie clenched her fists. "Look at them! They're so mean!"

"Are they the ones who scared Cookie?" Becky asked. Maddie had told her how scared Cookie had been.

Maddie nodded. "They're horrible."

Becky pushed open Josh's gate, glaring at the cats. "Come on! Don't you think we should make Josh help us look?"

"I suppose so," Maddie faltered. She shook herself. "Yes, he should."

"Come on, then," said Maddie's dad.

Maddie stomped up the path and rang the doorbell. She was shocked when Josh's dad answered the front door. She'd been expecting Josh.

"Um…. We wondered…."

"Your cats chased her kitten away," Becky put in over Maddie's shoulder.

Maddie's dad nodded. "She's lost, I'm afraid. We haven't seen her since yesterday morning."

Josh's dad looked worried. "Josh did say something about Tiger and Tom having a fight with a new cat…."

Maddie nodded. "We think they had another fight, and she ran off."

"Oh, dear. Look, Josh has to go to his football game, but can we come and help you look afterward?"

"Thanks," Maddie told him, and the girls set off to search again.

Cookie twitched and wriggled in her sleep, then woke up with a jolt, her fur all on end. She stared around the thick bushes, searching for the strange creature that had been chasing her. It had been even bigger than Tiger and Tom. But the gloomy space under the branches was empty—just her and a few beetles. She'd only been dreaming.

She peered out from under the bushes into the overgrown yard, her whiskers twitching.

The house had been abandoned, and the yard was covered in brambles and weeds. Cookie shivered in the early morning chill. She was stiff all over. She wasn't used to sleeping outside. She hadn't meant to, either; she'd been planning to hurry home to Maddie. But the car had scared her so much, she'd crawled into this safe little hole and fallen into an exhausted sleep.

Now she had to get home. And Maddie would feed her, too. She was so hungry. It seemed like forever since she'd had anything to eat.

Cookie stood up, ready to creep out of her hiding place, but then she collapsed, meowing with pain as her paw seemed to double up underneath her. She tried again, putting her weight on her other front paw, but she could hardly move. Her injured paw was dragging painfully as she limped through the damp grass. She had to stop and rest every few steps, and her paw was hurting more and more now. Finally, Cookie sank down at the edge of the weedy gravel path. She couldn't go any further for a while.

She was frozen, her fur was soaked through from the dew, and she was aching all over.

How was she ever going to get home?

241

"If we don't find her soon, maybe we should make a poster." Becky said. They'd searched all down Maddie's road again, and gone around the park, and the maze of little streets between the park and school. Now they were going back down Becky's road.

Maddie swallowed. "Yes," she whispered. It made sense. They'd been searching all morning. But it seemed like admitting that Cookie was really lost. Lost Cat posters always made her so sad. She couldn't imagine seeing Cookie's photo stuck to posts and fences.

242

"Let's keep calling her for a little longer," she whispered. She rubbed her eyes to wipe away the tears, then shouted, "Cookie! Cookie!"

Curled up by the path, Cookie was startled out of her half-sleep. That was Maddie, she was sure! She struggled to get up, but she couldn't stand on her hurt leg at all now. What if Maddie didn't see her? The yard was so overgrown that Maddie might easily miss her. Cookie wailed desperately, a long, heartbroken meow.

On the other side of the road, Maddie stopped, almost bumping into Becky. "Did you hear that?"

"Yes! Do you think it was Cookie?"

Maddie's dad came running up the road. "Maddie, I think I heard—"

243

"I know! We did, too! Come on!" Grabbing Becky by the hand, Maddie hurried across the road. "It sounds like Cookie's in that yard!"

Becky nodded. "I think you're right. No one lives in that house anymore. It's really quiet. And spooky. I don't like walking past it. But it would be a good place to hide if she was scared."

Cookie could hear Maddie getting closer. She meowed desperately and wobbled down the path, dragging her useless leg.

"She's here!" Maddie flung the gate open. "Oh, Cookie, you're hurt! She can't walk, Dad."

"Did she get hit by a car?" Becky asked anxiously.

Maddie picked up Cookie, as gently

244

as she could. "I'm not sure. Her paw's hanging funny, but it's not bleeding. She's scratched, though, on her ears and nose. I knew Tiger and Tom had been after her again!"

"We'd better get her looked at by the vet," said Dad, taking out his phone.

Cookie lay on Maddie, purring faintly. Maddie had found her. Cookie rubbed her chin lovingly against Maddie's shirt. She wasn't leaving her, ever again.

Chapter Eight
Home Sweet Home

"Is she going to be all right?" Maddie asked, exchanging an anxious look with Becky. Becky had begged to come to the vet; she was desperate to know if Cookie was going to be okay.

The vet nodded slowly. "I think she's just torn a muscle in her leg. She probably jumped and landed badly. She just needs to rest it. And I'll clean up these scratches and give her an injection of antibiotics, just in case. You said she's had trouble with the neighbor's cats? Looks like she's had a hard time."

Maddie nodded. "She won't go outside because she's so scared. They even came in through her cat flap. I'm not sure she feels safe even inside the house now."

The vet glanced at his computer screen. "She is microchipped, isn't she?"

"Yes, we had it done with her vaccinations," Dad said. "Why?"

"There's a new kind of cat flap you can get—it's a little expensive, but it works with the microchip. So only your cat would be able to use it."

Maddie looked at Dad hopefully. "Can I have one of those for my

247

birthday, just a little early? Please?"

Dad was grinning. "Two months early? We might be able to do that."

"You can program it, too, so you can keep Cookie in at night, if you want," the vet added.

Maddie nodded. "Then if Josh and his dad agree to keep Tiger and Tom in some of the time, we could tell the cat flap only to let Cookie out when we know they're inside!"

"Was it two boys who were fighting her?" the vet asked. "Are they neutered? Boy cats can be rough, if they haven't been. It might be worth suggesting to their owner that he has that done for them."

"We'll talk to Josh's dad," Dad promised Maddie.

Maddie cradled Cookie in her lap. They'd gone to the vet in such a rush that they hadn't put her in the cat carrier.

"I'll drop you two off, and then I'll go and see if that big pet store by the supermarket has those special cat flaps," Dad said as he pulled in.

"Look, there's Josh and his dad!" Maddie got out, carrying Cookie.

"You found her!" Josh's dad hurried forward. "Is she okay?"

"She's hurt her paw, and we had to take her to the vet," Maddie explained.

"She's really scratched, too…." Josh's dad peered at Cookie's nose. "Was that our two?"

Maddie nodded. "I think so. Are Tiger and Tom neutered? The vet said maybe that would help. He gave us a pamphlet with information."

Becky gave the pamphlet to Josh's dad's. "Probably not," he said. "We didn't have them fixed. They were strays. They showed up at work, about three years ago, and I brought them home. They were only tiny—about the size of your little one."

"Ohh…." Somehow, knowing that Tiger and Tom had been stray kittens made Maddie feel less angry with them. And Josh and his dad. It wasn't as if they'd asked to be cat owners, and they'd never realized how important it was to have the cats neutered.

"We can try and keep them in sometimes, too, like you said," Josh put in suddenly.

"That would be wonderful," Maddie said gratefully. She brushed her cheek lightly over Cookie's soft head. It was all going to be okay. She should call Kate to tell her what had happened. It was a nice thought. It didn't make her feel teary, like it would have done a couple of days ago. She missed Kate. But it wasn't as bad anymore, somehow....

"I guess I'd better get home," Becky said as they reached Maddie's.

"Can you stay for a little while?" Maddie asked. "That's okay, isn't it?"

she added to her mom, who had come out into the yard and was looking anxiously at Cookie. "It's good news, Mom. The vet says she probably just tore a muscle."

"Of course you can stay, Becky. Call your mom. Is Cookie really all right?" Maddie's mom petted Cookie gently. "Oh, she's purring."

Maddie beamed. "She is! She must be feeling better now that she's home."

"Maddie!"

Maddie looked around and saw Becky racing across the playground toward her. "How's Cookie?"

"Much better," Maddie said happily.

"She walking again now. She's has a little limp, but it's not too bad."

"I bet you're watching her like a hawk." Becky laughed.

"I love spoiling her," Maddie admitted. She looked at Becky shyly. "Mom said I could ask you over, so you can see how she is."

Becky beamed. "Really? Yes, please! Can I come today? Just to pop in and see her on the way home?"

"Yes, of course." Maddie could feel her face turn pink. She hadn't been sure if Becky would be as friendly at school as she had been over the weekend.

"Do you think Mrs. Melling would let you move tables, now that Kate isn't here anymore?" Becky asked thoughtfully. "There's space for you to sit with me and Lara and Keri."

"I guess we could ask," Maddie said, turning even more pink.

"Cool." Becky pulled her over to the small group of girls she'd been talking to. "Do you have a picture of Cookie in your bag to show everyone?"

"She looks different," Becky said thoughtfully later that afternoon, as the girls sat in Maddie's kitchen, watching Cookie sleeping in her basket.

254

"The scratches don't look as bad," Maddie suggested.

"No, it isn't that. I think she just looks happier. She must have been feeling miserable on Saturday." Becky glanced at the door. "Did your dad get that special cat flap?"

"Yes. And then he talked to Josh's dad about when Cookie gets to go outside. Josh's dad said that he called the vet, and Tiger and Tom are scheduled for Wednesday. Once they're neutered, the vet said he was sure they'd be less fierce."

"That's amazing." Becky grinned. "Aren't you glad I made you ring their bell? Oh, look! Cookie's awake!"

Cookie opened her eyes and yawned, showing her raspberry-pink tongue.

Then she looked lovingly at Maddie, and stepped out of her basket and on to Maddie's lap. She gave Becky a curious stare.

"Can I pet her?"

Maddie nodded. "She doesn't seem as jumpy as she did before. It can't really be the new cat flap, because she hasn't even been out yet."

"Maybe she's just glad to be home," Becky suggested.

Maddie smiled at Cookie. She seemed to be going back to sleep again, just on a warmer, cozier sort of bed.

Cookie burrowed deeper into Maddie's school sweater, and purred softly with each breath. She was safe now. And she wasn't frightened anymore.

The
Stray
Kitten

Contents

For Sophie

Chapter One
The Barnyard Kittens

"Are we going past the farm today?" Rosie asked her grandma hopefully. They had a few different ways back from school to Grandma's house, but the road past the farm was Rosie's favorite. Grandma wasn't usually in a rush, and she didn't mind walking slowly while Rosie stopped to look at any cats she happened to meet on the way. Rosie loved cats and was desperate for one of her own, but she hadn't managed to persuade her mom yet.

Grandma smiled at her. "Oh, I suppose we could go that way. I need to pick up some eggs from Mrs. Bowen. I might make a cake tonight, as it's the weekend." She looked down at Rosie and said thoughtfully, "But you know how she likes to chat, Rosie. Are you sure you won't get bored?"

Rosie looked up at her in surprise, and realized that Grandma was teasing. Grandma knew that Rosie loved going to the farm, because Rosie could go and watch the stray cats in the barnyard. There were lots of them, and Grandma said they were called feral cats because they weren't anyone's pets. Rosie had never managed to count them all, but she thought there were probably about 20 of them. Mrs. Bowen put food out occasionally, but mostly they lived on the mice they caught in the barn.

Rosie loved to imagine that the cats belonged to her, but they weren't really very friendly. If she sat on the foot step of the old rusty tractor for a while, they might prowl past her, but none of them would come to be petted.

One of the prettiest cats, a tabby with beautiful spotted markings, had given birth to a litter of kittens about five weeks before. Rosie had heard them meowing in the barn, but she hadn't been able to see them for a while, as the tabby cat had hidden them under some old hay bales that were stored in there.

Now the kittens were all running around the barnyard, and they weren't quite as shy as the older cats. Rosie was hoping that she could tame one of them. She couldn't help dreaming of taking a kitten home for her own pet.

She knew which one she wanted—the gorgeous little orange girl kitten. The kitten was so sweet—she had orangey-creamy fur with darker orange stripes, and a bright pink nose. Her eyes were green and very big, and Rosie thought she was the prettiest cat she'd ever seen.

Sometimes people called Rosie Ginger because of her long, curly red hair. Mom had always told her that her red hair was pretty and different, and that she'd like it when she was older, but Rosie wasn't so sure. Then she had seen the kitten. Rosie felt like she and the kitten were a pair, with their beautiful coloring. They were proud of it!

She wished the kitten would let Rosie pet her. Rosie could just imagine how soft her fur would be. The other day the kitten had come close enough to sniff at Rosie's fingers, but she'd darted off again without letting Rosie touch her.

Grandma called hello at Mrs. Bowen's door, and Rosie looked eagerly around the barnyard. She had something special for the cats today, and she was really hoping she could tempt the tabby kitten to come over to her. Rosie had noticed at lunch that her friend Maya had ham. Mom usually gave Rosie peanut butter and jelly, because that was her favorite, but she couldn't help thinking that the kitten would love Maya's sandwiches. Maya had been picking at the ham with a bored expression.

"Don't you like your sandwiches?" Rosie had asked, a plan starting to form in her mind.

"I wanted peanut butter, but my brother ate it all," Maya had sighed. "I hate ham...."

"Do you want to trade? I only have one left, but it's peanut butter and jelly," Rosie had offered hopefully.

"You sure?" Maya had looked delighted. "I didn't know you liked ham. You can have both of them!"

Rosie had slowly eaten one of the sandwiches, and then tucked the other one away in her lunch box.

Maya had watched her put it away.

"Didn't you like it?" Maya asked.

Rosie had leaned over closer to her. The kitten felt like a special secret, and she didn't want everyone to know. "I'm saving it. Remember the pretty tabby kitten I was telling you about that lives on the farm near my grandma's house? She came right up to me the other day, and I bet if I had some food she might even let me pet her. You don't mind, do you?"

Maya had shaken her head. "Of course not! Oh, you're so lucky, going to see kittens. Are they tiny?"

"The lady who owns the farm thinks they're about five weeks old. They're so cute! Maybe your mom would let you come home with us and see them

270

one day. I'm sure Grandma wouldn't mind."

Now at the farm, Rosie unwrapped Maya's sandwich, and started to crumble it into little bits, very gently, trying to keep as still and quiet as she could. It didn't take long for the cats to get a whiff of the delicious, meaty smell.

Rosie caught a movement out of the corner of her eye, just a streak of black fur. It was one of the kittens, peeking its head around the tractor wheel. Suddenly, several more little cat faces popped up, their whiskers twitching as they sniffed the air.

Rosie threw a bit of sandwich on the ground, and the closest kitten, the black one, pounced and swallowed it whole. Then he looked up for more. All the other kittens padded a few steps forward, not wanting to miss out. This time Rosie dropped the food closer, and one of the tabby kittens darted in and grabbed it, running back to a safe distance before she dared to stop and eat.

Rosie's heart thumped with delight as she saw her favorite orange kitten patter across the yard, eager to join in. Rosie tried to throw the next piece close to her, but the tabby kitten got there first and gobbled it up. The orange kitten gave Rosie a pitiful stare. *I'm so hungry*, the kitten seemed to be saying. *Pllleeeease feed me....*

This time Rosie threw her an extra-large piece. The orange kitten held it down with one paw, and hissed protectively when the others circled around her. Rosie laughed—the kitten's face was so funny—and the others looked up at Rosie, their eyes wide. Then they all ran back to their hiding places.

"Oh, no!" Rosie muttered, wishing she hadn't been so noisy.

But the orange kitten had only run a couple of steps away from her piece of sandwich, and now she eyed it uncertainly. Food—but also the noisy girl. What should she do? She eyed Rosie. She'd seen the girl before. The girl didn't usually make any noise, and she was quiet now. She wasn't even moving. And she still had lots more of that sandwich.

The kitten darted over and gulped down her piece, then looked around. Her brother and sisters were still hiding. If she went closer, while they weren't here, she might get *more* sandwich.... Nervously, ready to run just in case, the kitten edged closer, her eyes on the ham.

Rosie carefully tossed her a little bit, much closer to Rosie's feet this time.

The kitten stared at her suspiciously. Rosie looked back. Maybe it was too close. But then the kitten moved one paw forward, then the other, and then she was just close enough. The kitten started to gobble the sandwich, one eye on Rosie.

When it was gone the kitten sat up, licking her whiskers. She cast a quick look behind her. The others were all watching, but they weren't coming any closer. The food was all hers! She knew it was risky, but the sandwich was too delicious. She had to have more!

Rosie couldn't help smiling. The kitten was only about three feet from Rosie, almost close enough to touch. Instead of throwing the sandwich, Rosie held out her hand with the last pieces in it.

The orange kitten stared at Rosie nervously. What was she supposed to do now? The smell of that sandwich was so good. She could run up and grab it. So she skittered forward, her whiskers trembling, and quickly licked up a few crumbs from Rosie's hand, before stepping back to watch her again.

Then the kitten heard a noise and looked around. Her brother and sisters were starting to creep closer! They'd seen that she wasn't afraid, so they were getting braver, too. If she didn't wolf that sandwich down fast, she might have to share it.

The orange kitten hurried back to Rosie and started to eat as fast as she could, licking the crumbs away with her rough little tongue. Rosie had to try hard not to giggle—the kitten was tickling her!

Soon, the kitten had eaten it all. She glared at Rosie's hand, obviously wondering when it was going to produce some more.

"Sorry, it's all gone," Rosie whispered. "But I'll bring you some more next time. I bet Mom would let me have ham sandwiches if I asked, and I'll give them all to you."

The kitten eyed her expectantly, and Rosie stretched out her hand. The kitten licked it, but there was no more ham.

Rosie gently petted the top of the kitten's head, and the kitten jumped in surprise, looking up with huge emerald eyes. *What was that for?* she seemed to be saying. Rosie guessed she wasn't used to being petted. It made Rosie feel sad.

"Rosie! Where are you?" It was Grandma, calling from the farmhouse door. The orange kitten raced for the safety of the barn at top speed, chasing after her brother and sisters, and Rosie sighed as she got up. Still, she had managed to pet the orange kitten! She was so little and thin, but her fur had been so soft, exactly as she'd imagined. More than ever, Rosie wanted a kitten just like her....

Chapter Two
Change at the Farm

Rosie thought about the orange kitten all weekend. It was such a big step that the kitten had let Rosie pet her! Maybe she really would be able to tame the kitten. She was young, after all.

Rosie sat at the kitchen table, drawing pictures of the kitten while Mom made a shopping list. It was so hard to get the stripes right, and she had to keep starting again.

"That's beautiful, Rosie!" Mom said, leaning over.

Rosie shook her head. "Her face is more of a peachy color. I don't have the right pen for it."

"Is it a real cat?" Mom asked. "One of the ones you see on the way home from school?"

"She's a kitten at Mrs. Bowen's farm," Rosie explained. "You know, the little farm down the road from Grandma's house? There are five of them altogether. You'd love them, Mom."

Rosie looked hopefully at her mother. Maybe if Mom came and saw how cute the kittens were, she'd let them take the little orange one home. If only Rosie could tame her....

"She does look cute," her mom agreed. "Just be careful, though. Those wild cats probably have all kinds of horrible illnesses."

Rosie sighed. That didn't sound very hopeful....

Rosie's mom couldn't understand why Rosie was so excited to get to school on Monday morning.

"What's gotten into you, Rosie? Usually it's me telling you to get a move on, not the other way around."

Rosie just smiled. The sooner she was at school, the sooner it would be time to go home, and she could persuade Grandma to take her to the farm again. She just couldn't wait to get there.

She'd made sure Mom bought ham for her sandwiches this week, and she'd begged for an extra yogurt so she could save both sandwiches and not have her tummy rumbling all afternoon.

Luckily, Grandma didn't mind going to the farm again. Rosie ran ahead as they went down the road that led past the farm, calling to her grandma to hurry.

"I can't walk any faster, Rosie," said Grandma. "You really do love those cats, don't you?" She frowned a little as she said it, but Rosie was thinking about whether the orange kitten would remember her and didn't notice.

It seemed to Rosie that the cats appeared more quickly this time when she sat down on the old tractor. They remembered her as the food person. The orange kitten was the first to appear, her wide, white whiskers twitching with anticipation. Rosie wished the kitten wasn't so nervous, and that she could bring her home and take care of her. Rosie crumbled the sandwich and scattered a few pieces around, hoping the kitten would be brave enough to come close.

The orange kitten sniffed the air. More ham! The others weren't as brave, so she could have most of it to herself. She was sure the girl wasn't dangerous—she *had* touched her last time, but very gently. It had been quite nice. She'd even let the girl pet her again, if there was ham.

Rosie watched hopefully as the orange kitten crept forward, and she held out a particularly yummy-looking piece of ham. The kitten nibbled it delicately, then bumped Rosie's hand with her forehead, as if to say thank you. Rosie held out her left hand with more sandwich, and carefully rubbed behind the kitten's ears with the other.

The kitten looked up at her, still confused about why the girl wanted to pet her like this, but not minding too much. She even purred a little. Her ears were itchy, and the girl was rubbing the right spot.

The orange kitten finished the last of the sandwich and stared at Rosie, sniffing her fingers to see if more food would appear. When it didn't, the kitten yawned, showing her pink tongue, and jumped on her sister's tail, starting a kitten wrestling match.

Rosie watched them, giggling quietly to herself. They were so funny! Maybe tomorrow she would bring a piece of string for them to chase. She was sure they would like that.

The kittens suddenly scattered, and Rosie turned to see her grandma coming out of the farmhouse and waving good-bye to Mrs. Bowen. Grandma looked worried, and Rosie jumped up.

"What's the matter?" Rosie asked, as they headed toward the road.

Grandma looked at her and sighed. "I've been meaning to talk to you about this for a while, Rosie," she said. "Mrs. Bowen is moving—she's going to live with her son in town. The farmhouse is a bit too big for her now that she's on her own."

Rosie stared up at Grandma in surprise. She couldn't imagine the farm without Mrs. Bowen. "Oh. So who's going to live at the farm now?" she asked. "Is Mrs. Bowen selling it?" There was no For Sale sign up.

"No...," Grandma said. "Well, yes, I guess she is. The land has been sold to a developer—they're going to knock down the farm buildings and put up some houses instead. Mrs. Bowen signed the contract with them a little while ago, and she's been gradually packing her things up and moving them over to her son's house. She's leaving the farm this week."

Rosie gasped. It was all happening so quickly. Then a horrible thought struck her. "But Grandma, what's going to happen to the cats? They won't stay around when the farm's a building site! Where will they go?"

"It's all right, Rosie," Grandma said, putting an arm around her shoulders. "Mrs. Bowen has asked the people from the rescue shelter to find homes for the cats. They're going to come and get them tomorrow, she told me.

It'll be much better for the cats, you know. They'll check them out, and find good homes for the kittens. As for the older cats, they'll try and find someone with farm buildings or stables who'll keep them as outdoor cats, like they are here."

Rosie nodded. "But I won't see them anymore," she said sadly, her voice quivering. "Not even the little orange kitten, and she was starting to like me, Grandma, she really was. I ... I even thought of trying to take her home, if I could persuade Mom...."

"I'm not surprised she liked you, considering you were feeding her your sandwiches." Grandma smiled at her. "Mrs. Bowen does have windows, Rosie!"

"Oh." Rosie looked at Grandma, her cheeks a little pink. "You won't tell Mom, will you?" she asked.

"Well, no. But I think you'd have been better off eating the sandwiches yourself and buying some cat treats with your money," Grandma suggested.

"I don't think your mother would like to know she was making sandwiches for a tribe of wild cats."

"It won't matter now anyway," Rosie said tearfully. "I'll never see any of them again!"

When Mom picked Rosie up from Grandma's that night, she was surprised by the quiet, sad little figure who came down the stairs.

"What's up, Rosie? Did you have a bad day at school?" she asked.

Rosie shook her head.

"Go and get your things, Rosie," Grandma said, and by the time Rosie had packed up her homework and her pencil case, Grandma had obviously told Mom what was going on, because she didn't ask again.

Rosie stared miserably out the car window as they drove back to their house. The rescue shelter people would be thinking about new homes for the kittens already, she supposed. Rosie wondered who would get to adopt the orange kitten. Maybe it would be a girl her age. But no matter who it was, Rosie was sure no one would ever love the kitten as much as she did. She was so jealous.

Suddenly, Rosie sat up straight, staring out of the front window in excitement. Why shouldn't that girl be her? The kitten needed a new home, and she already liked Rosie. She could name the kitten Ginger!

Now Rosie would have to persuade her mom, of course.

"What is it, Rosie?" her mom asked. "A rabbit didn't run in front of the car, did it? I didn't feel anything."

"What? No! Mom, can we have a kitten?" Rosie begged. "Please? All of Mrs. Bowen's cats need homes. Please can we?"

Mom didn't say anything for a minute, and Rosie stared at her hopefully. At least she hadn't said no right away.

"I don't know, Rosie," Mom said. "It would be nice to have a pet—but those kittens are wild. They aren't used to people. I don't know if we'd be the right home. Someone who knows more about cats would be better, I think."

"We could learn about cats!" Rosie pointed out eagerly. "And those kittens really, really need homes, Mom. The rescue shelter people are coming to get the cats tomorrow. They'll hate being in cages. There's one of the kittens, Mom, who's really sweet, and she's already almost tame. She lets me pet her and she even eats out of my hand. She'd be a wonderful pet!"

"Well, I'll think about it. Maybe we could go and see how tame they really are. I'm not sure I want a wild kitten climbing my curtains...."

Rosie beamed. She was sure that Ginger was hers already. The kitten was so cute that Mom just wouldn't be able to resist her!

Back at the farm, the orange kitten curled up next to her mother and brother and sisters in a pile of hay in the old barn. It made a cozy nest, and she licked her paw sleepily. She was thinking about that girl, and wondering if she would come back tomorrow. She might bring more food, and maybe she would pet her fur again. It was nice when she did, like her mother licking her ears.

The kitten snuggled closer to her tabby sisters and closed her eyes. The hay was soft and warm, and she quickly fell asleep, never dreaming that everything was about to change.

Chapter Three
The Mystery Van

The next morning, the kittens were startled awake by a vehicle driving into the yard. Mrs. Bowen didn't have a car, and she took most of her eggs to town to sell, so very few people drove up to the farm. The kittens blinked at each other, then peered blearily over the edge of their nest. The kittens' mother, the spotted tabby cat, went to stick her nose around the old barn door. The orange kitten followed, eager to see what was going on. She wriggled between her mother's front paws, staring out into the yard.

Mrs. Bowen was standing by the back of a van, next to two girls. One of the girls opened up the doors and started to unload some boxes. The van smelled strange, the kitten thought. She'd never smelled anything quite like it before. And what were those wire box things?

Her mother was tense beside her, her whiskers pricked out as she watched what was going on. The kitten's brother and sisters were starting to meow, as they smelled the fear scents on their mother and the other older cats who were watching, too. They just didn't trust humans. The tabby cat backed into the barn so that her orange baby wasn't between her paws anymore, and butted the kitten hard with her nose.

The orange kitten looked around in surprise. What was wrong? Was this a game? Then she saw that her mother's eyes were wide with fear, and the fur had risen all along her back. This was no game. The mother swiped the kitten with her paw, sending her into the yard, and then she hissed at her with her ears laid flat. It was quite clear what she was telling her kitten to do.

Run!

The orange kitten scooted quickly out the barn door, heading for the old tractor. The tire had come away from the wheel, and the orange kitten had found this wonderful hiding place while she was playing. There she waited, her heart thudding with fear, trying to figure out what was going on.

Her mother had darted back into the barn to try and fetch her brother and sisters, and some of the other cats were trying to make a run for it, too. But as soon as they'd seen that the cats knew they were there, the two girls had quickly put a net around the barn door. Now they'd put on gloves, and they were catching the cats with strange things around the neck.

Ginger watched in horror as one by one her brother and sisters were caught and placed into wire cages. She could hear them meowing frantically as the cages were loaded into the van. Then one of the girls walked right up to the tractor where she was hiding.

The kitten edged back as far as she could go, trembling. She didn't want the girl to see her, but now *she* couldn't see what was happening. Where were they taking her brother and sisters? Were they all in that horrible-smelling van? Had they caught her mother, too? Her tail thrashed from side to side as the girl walked past, searching—for her, maybe. Ginger curled herself into a ball, her eyes wide with fear.

"I just caught the last one. I'm glad I had my gloves. She was struggling like anything!" shouted a voice from across the barnyard. Ginger then listened as the girl walked away from the tractor and the van doors slammed shut.

As the van drove off, a small bright-pink nose peeked out from the wheel of the tractor. Ginger watched the van rattling out of the farm gate, carrying her brother and sisters away from her, and gave a miserable little meow. Should she try to follow them? But she was sure her mother hadn't been happy about where they were going. Where was her mother? Maybe she would come and get her now that the people were gone. Or should she try to find her mother?

Ginger crept out of her hiding place and searched the yard. There was no sign of any other cats at all. But she couldn't believe that her mother had left her. She wouldn't! Even if they had caught her, she would have gotten away somehow.

Ginger wandered around the outside of the barn, meowing sadly, and wishing her mother would come back soon, because she was hungry. Maybe she'd gone hunting for a mouse for breakfast. Yes, that was it.

As the morning wore on, Ginger got hungrier. She searched around for her mother and meowed pitifully for her, but still she didn't come.

At last she went a little closer to the farmhouse, drawn by the smell from the garbage cans. Mrs. Bowen had cleaned out her fridge and cupboards, and there were some black plastic bags lying there. The kitten pawed at one of them hopefully and clawed a little hole, grabbing some old cheese. She nibbled at it. It wasn't great, but it was better than nothing.

She ate all of it, her whiskers twitching at the strange taste. She wished the girl would come back and feed her more of that delicious ham. She had been surprised when the girl had petted her, but she'd liked it. If the girl came back now, Ginger wouldn't be on her own. If only *somebody* would come!

Rosie practically dragged Grandma to the farm after school.

"All right, Rosie, all right! But we can't stay long. Mrs. Bowen is still packing. She's moving tomorrow. She won't want us bothering her today," Grandma said firmly.

"I know, but I need to find out about the kittens, whether the people came today. Mom said we could stop by the rescue shelter on the way home!" Rosie looked up at her grandma with shining eyes. "If she likes Ginger, we could even take her home this afternoon!"

Grandma smiled. It was great to see Rosie so excited, although she wasn't sure Rosie's mom would agree to a kitten right away.

Mrs. Bowen waved to them from the kitchen window. She was piling china carefully into a big box, and looked a bit hot and tired.

"Did they come?" Rosie asked her excitedly. "Did they take all the kittens to the rescue shelter?"

Mrs. Bowen smiled. "Oh, yes, dear. This morning."

"Do you have the address?" Rosie asked hopefully. "Mom says we can look at the kittens—she might even let me keep one of them! The sweet little orange one, you know?"

Mrs. Bowen wrote it down, and Rosie folded the piece of paper and tucked it carefully in her pocket.

Mom had said she'd try to leave work early so they could go to the rescue shelter that evening, and now Rosie sat by Grandma's front window, watching for her car. When her mom arrived at last, she dashed out to meet her.

"The kittens are at the shelter! I've got the address, Mom. Come on, they're only open until six!" she cried.

Her mom laughed. "All right! But remember, we're just looking. I know you want to take that kitten home, but I still need to think about this. Anyway, I can't imagine we'll be allowed to take one of them yet. They'll need to be checked by a vet to make sure they're healthy."

Rosie nodded. "But at least let's go and see!" she pleaded.

Secretly, she was sure that as soon as her mom saw Ginger, she would give in. Maybe they wouldn't be able to take her home today, but they could still tell the rescue shelter people that they wanted her!

311

The rescue shelter was in the next town. The girl at the reception desk knew about the kittens, and she smiled at Rosie's eager questions.

"I'm sure you can go and see them," she said. "We wouldn't usually let people visit the kittens until we'd checked them out, but since you already know them...." She led Rosie and her mom to a room at the back, with large cages in it.

Rosie spotted the tabby mother cat at once. She was prowling up and down the cage, looking anxious.

"Oh, she really doesn't like being shut in. And she must be upset that she's not with her kittens," Rosie said sadly.

The girl from the rescue shelter nodded. "I know. But because she's a feral cat, we need to separate her kittens from her now. It's so the kittens can get used to humans and give them the best chance of settling in at their new homes. They're in that cage at the end. Want to see them?"

"Oh, yes. Come and see, Mom!" Rosie whispered, grabbing her mom's hand and pulling her along.

"Oh, they are sweet!" her mom agreed, peering through the wire. "Look at that little black one!"

But Rosie was staring anxiously into the cage. There were four kittens in the basket, curled up asleep—one black, and three tabbies. There was no pretty little orange kitten.

Ginger wasn't there!

Chapter Four
Looking for Ginger

"Don't cry, Rosie," Mom said as they walked back to the car.

Rosie was trying not to cry, but there were just a few tears that she couldn't seem to stop. She was thinking about what could've happened at the farm when the cats were caught.

Why hadn't Ginger been with them? Probably she'd found a way out of the barn and slipped away. But why? Maybe she'd been scared of the rescue shelter people, but it was also possible that Ginger had stayed behind to wait for her. Maybe Ginger hadn't wanted to go because of Rosie, because Rosie had been feeding her and playing with her.

Rosie had read about feral cats on the internet and knew that they were good hunters, but Ginger was too young to hunt for herself. Her mother would still have been catching food for her kittens. Without her mother to feed her, she might starve. Rosie nodded firmly. She had to go back to the farm. She just had to find Ginger, no matter how long it took.

Rosie was determined to look for the kitten the next day, but she and Grandma were shocked when they reached the farm. Grandma had come another way to get Rosie from school, and they both stopped in surprise as they came close.

"My goodness, that went up so quickly!" Grandma exclaimed.

A huge wire fence was now surrounding the barnyard, covered in big notices about wearing hard hats, and no children playing on the building site. It was a building site already!

Rosie pressed her face up against the wire fence. The barnyard was deserted, with no sign of life at all.

"Can't we go in and look for her?" she asked Grandma.

"No, Rosie. Look—it says no one can go in. We'll just have to keep coming by and hope we see her— or maybe we could ask the builders to keep an eye out. There's no one here now, but I'm sure there will be soon; otherwise they wouldn't have bothered to put the fence up, would they?"

Grandma was right. The next day, a couple of men in yellow hard hats were wandering around the building site with a little machine that beeped. It took Grandma and Rosie forever to catch the men's attention, but at last one of them came over.

"Yes?" he asked.

"Have you seen a kitten?" Rosie said nervously. "There were some cats here, and they were taken to a rescue shelter, but we think one of the kittens ran away...." She trailed off. "We just wondered if you'd seen her? An orange kitten?"

"No, sorry." The builder turned away. Rosie didn't dare call him back, even though she wanted to.

"Could you keep an eye out for her, please!" Grandma called, and Rosie squeezed her hand gratefully. She'd wanted to ask that, too.

They continued walking, Rosie looking back sadly every so often. They seemed to be able to see that fence no matter how far away they were.

"Don't give up hope, Rosie," Grandma told her. "You never know."

But Rosie couldn't help feeling that her chances of finding Ginger were getting smaller and smaller. What if she had escaped before the fence went up? Maybe Ginger wasn't there at all!

Ginger was hiding between two hay bales in the barn, peering out occasionally, and trembling as the men's heavy boots thumped past the door. Who were they? And why were they stamping and crashing around her home? She wished her mother and her brother and sisters would come back, but she was sure now that they were gone forever. If her mother had still been here, she would have come to find her by now, wouldn't she?

Ginger had hidden in the barn when the men put the fence up, and she'd dashed back there again this morning. She didn't dare do more than poke her nose out a bit occasionally to see if they were gone. She was starving, and it was getting harder to find anything to eat in the garbage bags by the farmhouse.

There were voices outside now. Were more people coming? She wanted the farm to go back to being quiet and safe like it was before. Ginger listened miserably, but then her ears pricked up. She knew that voice. It was the girl! She was there! Maybe she'd known Ginger was hungry and had brought her some more sandwiches! Ginger edged nervously around the barn door, the fur on her back ruffling up.

The men were still there, and the girl was talking to one of them. If only they would go, Ginger could run over to the girl. Ginger meowed a tiny meow, hoping the girl would hear. The kitten didn't dare call loudly in case the men saw her.

No! The girl was leaving!

Rosie walked sadly down the road with Grandma, leaving the kitten staring desperately after her.

The girl was gone, and Ginger didn't know if she would come back. Ginger felt so small and scared, and very, very alone....

Chapter Five
Parting Ways?

On Friday, Grandma was waiting outside school for Rosie as usual. It was raining, and Rosie was taking a while. She and Maya were among the last few to come out, and Maya had her arm around her friend.

"Rosie's really upset about Ginger," she explained to Rosie's grandma.

"I just don't think I'm ever going to

see her again," Rosie whispered sadly.

"You can't give up!" Maya said firmly.

Maya's mom had come up and was giving Rosie a concerned look. "Is everything okay, Maya?" she asked, and Maya explained about Ginger being missing.

"Poor little thing," her mom muttered. "Have you tried putting food out to tempt her, just in case she's still around?"

Rosie lifted her head. "No, we haven't. We should try that! Can we do that today, Grandma? Oh, I should have saved my sandwiches for her!"

"You could buy some cat treats at the pet store!" Maya suggested.

"Sammy loves those, especially the salmon-flavored ones."

"Please!" Rosie begged. "I'll pay you back, Grandma."

Grandma smiled. "I think we can get some cat treats. Come on."

"I wish I could come with you, but I have dance class," Maya said. "I'd love to see Ginger. I bet she'll come out for those cat treats."

"Thanks for the great idea," Rosie told her gratefully, and she and Grandma set off for the pet store.

"Call me and let me know if you see her!" Maya yelled after them, and Rosie turned back to wave. Maya had understood why she was so upset. She adored her fluffy white cat, Sammy. He'd been lost for a couple of days last year, and it had been awful.

Rosie chose the salmon treats, like Maya had suggested. Sammy was handsome and liked his food. Ginger was sure to like them, too.

They walked quickly over to the farm. Down the road, they could hear banging and the rumbling sounds of big vehicles. Rosie and Grandma exchanged a look and sped up to see what was going on.

The farm looked so different. The builders were knocking down the barn! A huge yellow digger was thundering past them on the other side of the fence—even Rosie felt scared by how big and loud it was. How would a kitten feel!

"Oh, no!" Rosie cried. "That's where the cats all used to sleep!" She watched as the digger tore at the walls. She clung to the fence, pressing her face against it so hard the wires marked her forehead, and looked frantically around the site. She couldn't see the kitten.

"Ginger isn't there, is she?" she asked, her voice shaking. "You don't think she was in the barn, when they started pulling it down...."

Grandma stared through the fence at the builders and their machines. "I don't know, Rosie. Ginger could be hidden because she's frightened. She might want to come out, but she doesn't dare." Grandma put her arm around Rosie.

"Try the cat treats," Grandma suggested gently. "Why don't you scatter a few through the fence? Maybe the smell will tempt her." She helped Rosie tear open the packet. "My goodness, I would think she could smell that from miles away. They're very fishy, aren't they?"

The treats did smell very strong, and Rosie pushed a few through the mesh of the fence. Then they waited, watching the builders in their bright yellow vests and hard hats as they cleared away the broken pieces of wood that were all that was left of the kitten's home. But there was no sign of Ginger—no long, white whiskers peeking out from behind a hay bale, no orange tail flicking around the corner of the farmhouse. The kitten was nowhere to be seen. After 10 minutes, Grandma turned to Rosie.

"It's starting to rain harder, Rosie. We'd better go, but we'll try again. Maybe your mom will bring you over tomorrow or on Sunday. We won't give up."

Rosie nodded, feeling slightly better. She would never give up on Ginger.

Even though she was only across the yard, Ginger hadn't seen the girl. The kitten was hiding under the abandoned tractor, shuddering each time the digger crashed through her old home. Ginger had run out as soon as the builders had come into the barn. She was wet, cold, and hungry, and now she didn't have anywhere to sleep!

Since the barn was destroyed, Ginger made a decision. This wasn't her home anymore. She realized now that her mother wasn't coming back. She needed to find somewhere new to live.

Maybe she could go and find that nice girl with the sandwiches?

Rosie's mom took her back to the farm on Sunday, and they stood by the fence calling for a long time.

"Put some more cat treats down," Mom suggested. "Then at least Ginger will have something to eat."

Suddenly, Rosie gasped. "Mom, look!"

"What is it? Did you see her? I can't see anything." Mom peered through the fence.

"No, that's it! I can't see anything. That's the point! The cat treats I put through the fence on Friday are gone!"

"Are you sure?" Mom asked.

"Definitely. I was right here, so they should be just on the other side of the fence. Ginger's been here. She's eaten them! Oh, Mom!" Rosie beamed at her, feeling so relieved. She bent down to empty some more cat treats out of the packet.

"Rosie, what's that?" Rosie looked up to see her mom pointing across the yard, down to the side of the farmhouse. "Can you see? It looks like something orange, by the garbage...."

Rosie jumped to her feet. Mom was right. Slipping along the side of the farmhouse was a flash of orange fur. It had to be Ginger!

But then the creature slunk out further into the yard, sniffing at the piles of wood from the barn. It was a fox, with a bright-white tail tip.

"Oh no…," Rosie breathed. It wasn't very big, but compared to a tiny kitten it was huge. "It might hurt Ginger, and oh, Mom, I bet it was the fox who ate the cat treats!"

Mom sighed and nodded. "I'm afraid it could have been, yes."

Sadly, they turned and walked away, Rosie blinking back tears. She had promised herself she wouldn't give up, but it was starting to look hopeless….

That evening, Rosie's mom was determined to cheer Rosie up. A television show they both liked was just about to start, and Mom hurried upstairs to get her.

"Rosie!" she called, opening her bedroom door. "Are you coming downstairs? Oh, Rosie!"

Rosie was sitting huddled on the floor, leaning against her bed.

"What's the matter?" Mom asked, sitting down on the floor beside her. "You're crying!"

"I'll never see Ginger again." Rosie sniffed. "What if she's hurt?" she whispered. "She might have been injured when the barn was knocked down. Maybe she got trapped. Maybe that fox ate her!" Tears rolled down Rosie's cheeks again.

"Ssshh, Rosie, don't say that." Mom hugged her close. "I don't think foxes normally attack cats. You're imagining the worst; the kitten might be fine. She's probably just staying hidden because she's afraid." She stroked Rosie's red hair. "You love this kitten, don't you? You've tried so hard to make friends with her—Grandma told me how patient you were, trying to get her to like you."

Rosie's mom hesitated. "Rosie, we could try adopting one of the other kittens at the rescue shelter…. What about the little black one?"

Rosie looked up, her eyes horrified and still teary. "We can't! We can't, Mom!"

"I mean, if we don't find Ginger," her mom explained gently.

Rosie shook her head. "Ginger's special," she said. "She's unique, too, like me. But it isn't just that. She seems so bright, and she's got so much bounce…."

She twisted one of her red curls around her finger, deep in thought. Ginger *was* special. And if she couldn't have Ginger, she didn't want another kitten.

Chapter Six
A Close Call

Ginger had felt brave when she decided to leave the farm and look for a new home. She had waited until all the people were long gone, and the farm was quiet. She would find somewhere comfortable. Maybe she'd find that friendly girl with the food.

But she hadn't realized that the

fence went all around the farm. It was very high, and it was struck down tight to the ground. Ginger couldn't get out! Scratching at it didn't work, and when she tried climbing it, she fell. At last she had slunk away to find a place to sleep. She'd hidden herself in Mrs. Bowen's woodpile, near the farmhouse. It wasn't comfortable, but it felt safe, far away from the builders' noisy, smelly machines.

The mice seemed to have been scared away by the men, too. Ginger had almost caught one, but the mouse had slipped into a hole, leaving Ginger hungrier than ever. It had seemed so easy when her mother did it. Ginger found some fishy-tasting round things by the fence over the last couple of days, but they hadn't filled her up. She'd seen a fox hanging around, and she had a feeling it had picked all the best pieces out of the garbage bags, because there was nothing left.

Now Ginger could feel herself growing weaker. Even though the rain leaked through into her woodpile nest and soaked her, she'd been grateful for it, as at least she wasn't thirsty. She'd been able to lap the water caught in the old buckets that were lying around the yard. But she needed food. She'd smelled delicious smells like the sandwiches the girl used to bring. They had been very good. She hoped the girl might come back, but probably she didn't like the big machines either, Ginger thought, as she drifted into a restless sleep.

Ginger was awakened by the smell of ham sandwiches. A builder had stopped for lunch and was sitting on one of the big logs. The smell was irresistible. Ginger uncurled herself and crept out. The sandwiches were in an open box next to the man. There was one left, and out of it trailed a piece of wonderful ham. She had to have it. Ginger looked up at the man. He was staring across the yard. He wouldn't notice, would he?

Ginger thrust a paw into the box, hooking the bread with her claws.

"Hey! Get out of there, you!" The man swiped at her with his hand! Ginger shot away, without even a morsel of bread to show for it. She raced up the tree that had been left standing in a corner of the yard by the fence, and crouched flat on one of the branches, quivering with terror. She looked down fearfully, digging her claws into the bark. She had never climbed a tree before, but instinct had taken her to the safest place. The man hadn't followed her.

Ginger stayed there for hours, too scared to move. By the middle of the afternoon, she felt it was safe to come down from the tree. It wasn't as easy as going up. She hadn't really *thought* about going up; she'd just done it.

She looked down from her branch—the ground seemed so far away.... She was stuck!

Rosie only got through school that day because Maya kept nudging her, reminding her that Mrs. Wilkinson was watching. Rosie would manage to listen or concentrate on what she was supposed to be doing for about five minutes before she started thinking about Ginger again.

Maya was coming to Grandma's today, and they were planning to look for Ginger together. Rosie was glad—Maya was so enthusiastic about looking for Ginger. Rosie had been disappointed so much that it was hard to keep her hopes up.

Maya jogged ahead as they came up to the farm. "Wow! It really is a building site. Oh, Rosie, poor Ginger. She must be really scared with all those people around, and those great big diggers. It's so noisy!"

Rosie nodded sadly and looked wearily through the fence into the yard. It looked so different now, with the barn gone and the yard covered in piles of rubble. Rosie wasn't expecting to see anything. But what was that in the tree over there? Rosie peered through the fence and grabbed Maya's sleeve.

"Maya! Grandma! Is that a cat in the tree? On that branch, there. No, no, there, look!"

A flash of orange fur showed among the leaves. It was hard to see if it was a cat, but *something* was moving.

"You could be right...," Maya said doubtfully. "I can't quite see."

Grandma was squinting through the fence. "I can't tell, either...."

"I am right! I know I am!" Rosie looked at them eagerly. "She's there, she really is. Yes, I can see her stripes! Oh, I can't believe it, I'd almost given up. Ginger! Ginger! I don't think she can hear me, with all this noise." She frowned. "Oh, Grandma, she must be so scared with all this going on. We have to get her out, we just have to!"

Rosie dashed along the fence, with Maya racing after her, and shouted to one of the men walking by. "Hey! Excuse me! Over here, please listen!"

But the man just walked past, pushing a wheelbarrow. He didn't even look at Rosie and Maya. Rosie rattled the gate, but no one seemed to hear her.

Grandma came up, looking anxious. "Rosie, calm down!"

"I can't make anyone listen!" Rosie looked at her wildly. "They have to let us in so we can go and get Ginger!"

Grandma pulled them gently away from the gate. "Girls, come back. It's a building site. I don't think they'll let us go in. Look, that man's coming out. We'll ask him." Grandma smiled politely at the man, who gave them a curious look.

"Excuse me, but have you seen a kitten around at all? She used to live on the farm, and she's disappeared. We think we might have just seen her in that tree."

The builder shook his head. He didn't look very interested. "No cats, sorry," he said, starting to shut the gate.

"She *is* there!" Rosie cried. "We've just seen her, we know she's there. You've knocked down her home, and you might have hurt her! You have to let us find her!"

The builder looked confused, and Grandma hugged Rosie tight. "Look, I'm sorry. The girls are very worried about the kitten. We really do think we saw her a minute ago. Could you please just keep an eye out for her?" She pulled an old receipt out of her bag and scribbled on it. "This is my phone number. If you could call us if you see her, we'd be so grateful."

The man took the note and stuffed it into the pocket of his reflective vest. Then he locked the gate, and walked off. Rosie watched him go, tears running down her nose. She was pretty sure he'd never look at the note again.

Grandma guided Rosie and Maya away from the gate. She was worried the builders might get annoyed and tell them to stop hanging around.

From in the tree, Ginger had heard the voices. It was the girl! The one with the food, who had petted her. The girl had come back for her. Ginger was sure that was why the girl was there. She tried desperately to get down the tree trunk.

But now the girl was going! Ginger meowed frantically, *please wait!* But no one heard her. Ginger took a flying leap from halfway down the tree trunk, and raced over to the fence.

Come back! Come back! I'm here!

But it was too late.

Chapter Seven
A Growing Friendship

When they got back to Grandma's house, Grandma made Maya and Rosie sit down and have a drink.

"You can't get so worked up, Rosie!" Grandma said. "You can't help that kitten if you're shouting at people and getting into trouble, can you?"

Rosie sighed. Grandma was right. "I just don't think he was even listening,

Grandma," she said sadly. "That's why I was so angry. That man just said no cats, without even thinking about it!"

"But you saw her, Rosie!" Maya put in. "Ginger is still there! That's really good news! That was your orange kitten, wasn't it?"

Rosie smiled at last. "I'm sure, really sure. It was her pretty striped fur. I could see it through the leaves. She was up in that tree, I know she was. I wish she'd heard me, but it was just so noisy. I bet she would have come down, to see if I had sandwiches again." Rosie frowned. "I hope she wasn't stuck. That tree's enormous."

"Well, all we can do is go again tomorrow. As long as we're back in time for your mom to pick you up, I don't mind how long we stay. If we're there when the builders are gone, it'll be easier." Grandma smiled. "If she's there, we'll find her."

"Couldn't we go back now?" Rosie pleaded. "I'm not sure I can wait until tomorrow...."

Grandma shook her head. "It's getting late now, and you both still need to have a snack. We can go right after school tomorrow."

"Okay," Rosie sighed.

Ginger sat by the fence and howled. The girl had been here, and she'd missed her! Ginger scratched desperately at the fence, hoping to chase after the girl, but it didn't budge. She was still trapped.

Ginger trailed sadly back to the woodpile, avoiding the builders. At least the girl had come back. Maybe she'd come again tomorrow?

Rosie raced along the road, hardly hearing Grandma calling to her to slow down. She was desperate to get to the farm and see if Ginger was still there. At last she reached the fence by the tree. She wound her fingers through the wire, gazing hopefully up at the tree. There was no glint of orange fur. Rosie sighed. Still, she couldn't expect Ginger to be in exactly the same place she was yesterday.

Ginger is there, she told herself firmly. *You just need to look.*

Rosie tiptoed along the fence, trying to peer through. The awful thing was, Ginger might be asleep somewhere, just out of sight! She could miss her so easily.

Suddenly, Rosie gasped. It was as though all her breath had disappeared. Ginger was there! The kitten was crouched under the wheel of the old tractor, where Rosie used to tempt her with ham sandwiches. Ginger's ears were back, and she was watching the builders. Rosie's heart thudded as she saw how thin Ginger was.

Rosie crouched down by the fence. "Ginger!" she whispered, not wanting to scare the kitten, but of course Ginger

359

didn't hear her. Rosie tried again, a little louder, and Ginger's ears twitched.

"Ginger!" Rosie waved to her as well this time, and she saw Ginger's eyes widen. The kitten had seen her! She stood up slowly, cautiously, and crept across the yard toward Rosie, moving one paw at a time and glancing around fearfully.

Rosie's eyes filled with tears as she saw how scared Ginger was. "Hey, Ginger!" she whispered, as the kitten stopped in front of the fence.

Ginger stood hesitantly, staring at Rosie, and gave a very small meow. Had the girl come back for her?

"Oh, Ginger, I'm so glad to see you!" Rosie said. "Are you all right? You look okay, just really thin." She giggled. "I don't know why I'm asking you questions. It isn't as if you can answer...." Very slowly, Rosie reached into her bag. "Look, I've got your favorite." She opened up her lunch box, pulling out the sandwiches she'd saved. "Yummy ham, Ginger, come and see!"

Ginger ran toward her. The girl *had* come back! And she'd brought food. Ginger was still nervous, but the girl had always been gentle, and the food smelled too good to resist. Although Ginger was half-wild, she'd been used to Rosie feeding her from when she was tiny. Ginger sat on the other side of the fence and meowed hopefully.

"Here you go, it's okay," Rosie said, pushing pieces of sandwich through the fence. Ginger gobbled them down eagerly. "You look like you haven't eaten in a week," Rosie told her. Her eyes widened. "Actually, it *is* a week, isn't it? You must be starved. Here, have some more."

"Rosie, I can't believe you've already found her! I won't come closer in case I frighten her off, okay? I'll just stay back here." Grandma leaned against the fence on the other side of the road, watching Rosie and the kitten.

Ginger finished the sandwich and sniffed, looking for crumbs. The sandwich had helped, but she still felt hungry. She wondered if the girl had any more. Ginger looked at her uncertainly, and edged forward. The kitten was sniffing at Rosie's fingers. She even licked them, in case the girl tasted like ham, but she didn't.

Rosie giggled—her tongue was tickly—then scratched Ginger's ears. Rosie could only just reach—the holes in the fence were too small for her whole hand to go through. "How are we going to get you out?" Rosie muttered, as she stroked Ginger's head with one finger.

Ginger ducked her head shyly, rubbing herself against the wire. It was warm, she ate, and now someone she liked was fussing over her. She closed her eyes and started to purr, very quietly, her tiny chest buzzing.

Rosie could feel Ginger trembling with the purr as she leaned against the wire. Rosie almost felt like purring herself, and a huge smile spread over her face.

"She's purring!" Rosie whispered to Grandma. Rosie was just starting to wonder if she should call to a nearby builder, and ask him to pick Ginger up and bring the kitten out to her. They wouldn't want a kitten getting in their way….

Then the man tripped and dropped the bucket he was carrying. It hit the ground with a loud clang. Ginger leaped into the air in fright, and Rosie jumped, her heart thumping.

Ginger had disappeared, streaking across the yard in a panic, and Rosie looked anxiously around for her, clinging sadly to the wire fence. Ginger had trusted her—the kitten had enjoyed being petted, and now all that work was for nothing!

It wasn't Ginger's fault, but Rosie knew that Ginger was never going to let one of the builders pick her up. She'd run away from the girls from the rescue shelter, and that was before Ginger had had a week of scary builders invading her home.

Ginger would let Rosie feed her, and pet her. But Rosie was on one side of the fence, and Ginger was on the other. How was Rosie ever going to get the kitten out?

Chapter Eight
Coming Home

"Oh, Rosie, she was so close!" Grandma came hurrying over. "That was such bad luck. She really seemed to be trusting you." Grandma shook her head. "I just can't believe how patient you've been with her. You deserve to have her, Rosie, you really do."

Rosie gave her a grateful hug.

"Well, what are we going to do now?" Grandma wondered. "How on earth are we going to get Ginger out? She's too frightened to let anyone pick her up—you might just about be able to do it, but those builders can't let you go on to the site, even if they want to. If you hurt yourself, they could be in real trouble. I suppose we're just going to have to call the rescue shelter and get them to do it."

Rosie nodded. "I hadn't thought of the rescue shelter people coming back. They'd probably have to use a net or a cage, wouldn't they?" Rosie shuddered. "It's better than staying where she is. It's really dangerous here. But Ginger will be scared and run away again.... Oh, Grandma, there's got to be a better way!" Rosie sat down on the grass, thinking hard. "Well, I can't go in, so Ginger has to come out, doesn't she? But I just don't see how—this fence is like a prison, even for a cat."

Grandma sighed. "I have a feeling we're going to be here for a while." She patted Rosie on the shoulder. "You stay here and watch for her. I'll head home and make us some sandwiches. I won't be long." Rosie looked up suddenly. "Don't worry. I'll bring more ham for Ginger, too. But if we do catch that kitten, she'll need to learn to like something other than ham...."

Rosie watched her walk slowly down the road. She was so lucky having Grandma. If Grandma didn't have her after school, she'd never even have met Ginger. But mostly because Grandma was never in a rush. Grandma didn't mind spending an hour sitting outside a building site, watching for a kitten. That was pretty special.

Rosie turned back to the fence and stared at it hopelessly. If only she could climb over it! The builders were starting to leave now. Once they were gone, no one would see…. But Grandma would be really upset with her. She'd trusted Rosie to be sensible, leaving her here. Rosie couldn't let her down.

Rosie shook the fence, making it rattle. It was even taller than the one at school around the playing field. Then she stopped, and stared at the fence thoughtfully. The one at school had holes in, where people had leaned on it over the years, and one place where some of the older boys had decided to dig a tunnel underneath when they were bored.

Rosie couldn't get *over* the fence, but maybe she could get *under* it. Or at least the kitten could....

She crouched down and peered at the base of the fence. It ran along the ground, and it was held tightly between posts, so there were no gaps—yet. Rosie started to hunt for a likely place. Oh! Yes, here.... Something had already done half the job for her. Maybe that fox they'd seen before. Whatever it was had dug a hole a few inches deep under the fence before it gave up.

Rosie lifted the fence carefully. She was pretty sure that Ginger could fit under there, but she'd better dig it out a bit more, just to be certain. Rosie found a big stone and started to scrape the earth away as fast as she could, looking up every so often to check for Ginger.

The farm was quiet. Ginger's ears and whiskers stopped their panicky twitching at last. She poked her nose out from under the large black tarp where she'd dashed after that loud bang. No noise of diggers, no rumbling wheels, no men shouting. It should be safe now. Ginger slid out, still listening carefully. There was an odd scritch-scratching noise coming from across the yard. Was it that fox who'd been stealing from the garbage? She'd seen it again the other night.

There was no smell now, so it couldn't be a fox. Ginger padded slowly out into the yard, following the noise. It sounded like something was digging under the fence. Maybe it *was* that fox. The fur rose up on Ginger's back. She crept around the back of the tractor, and threw a quick look over at the fence.

It was her! The girl! She was still there! The noise hadn't scared her away. And she was digging under the fence. Was she trying to come in?

Ginger gave a hopeful meow, and crept across the yard toward Rosie, glancing around, just in case.

Rosie dropped the stone. "Ginger!" Rosie sat up on her heels eagerly, grabbing the fence to look through the wire, and Ginger paused, scared by the sudden movement. "Oh, I'm sorry...." Rosie rocked back on her knees, leaving a space between herself and the fence. "I didn't mean to scare you, Ginger. I'm just so glad to see you!" Rosie dug the last tiny handful of fishy cat treats out of the packet that she'd been keeping in her bag, and scattered them for Ginger— on Rosie's side of the fence.

"Come on, Ginger ... please...."

The tiny kitten sniffed thoughtfully. The smell was familiar. Those strange round things she'd found before! They were from the girl, too? Ginger preferred ham, but she wouldn't complain. Still, she had to get under the fence to get them.

Ginger padded closer, peering through the hole. It seemed big enough. She'd been hoping to find the girl, and a way out. Now the girl had made her one. Ginger stared up at Rosie, her big green eyes hopeful, and almost trusting. She would do it.

Rosie stared back, her eyes hopeful, too, desperate for Ginger to trust her. "Hey, little one," Rosie whispered. "Come on...."

Ginger crouched down, and started to wriggle under the fence, the wire just skimming the fur on her back. She popped out the other side, shook herself, and then sneezed from the dust. Then she eyed the cat treats eagerly.

"Go on, they're for you!" Rosie reassured her, and Ginger gobbled them down, a curious expression on her face. Such an odd flavor. But she could get used to it. Ginger licked her whiskers and looked up at Rosie. Then she put one tiny paw on her knee, and meowed.

More?

"Are you still hungry?" Rosie smiled. "You could come back to Grandma's with me. She's making ham sandwiches, your favorite." Rosie stood up slowly, and stepped backward. "You coming? Hmmm? Coming, Ginger?"

And Ginger padded after Rosie, her tail waving, following her home.

Out now:

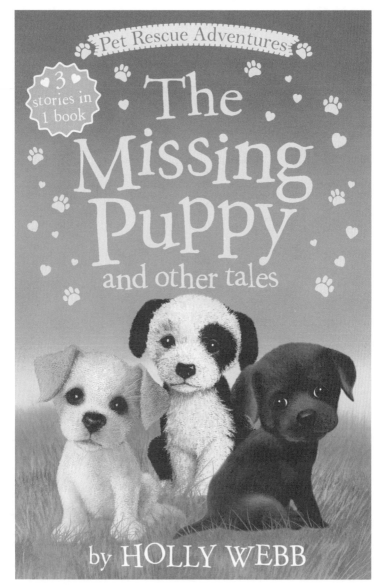

Pet Rescue Adventures

3 stories in 1 book

The Missing Puppy

and other tales

by HOLLY WEBB

Pet Rescue Adventures

Three heartwarming puppy
stories to treasure in one book, from
best-selling author Holly Webb.

Holly's True-life Tales

Milly

The Stag Beetle Hunter

Our new cat, Milly, has decided it's too boring
(or too much hard work?) to hunt mice or birds.
So far, her total haul is one frog and three stag
beetles, which are beetles found in Britain that
have huge, antler-like pincers. But at least one of
the stag beetles fought back and got her with its
pincers, which I think she deserved....

Sammy

The Mushrooms

My husband and I adopted two kittens when we moved into our first house—Sammy (Sampson, named after the cat in the "Church Mice" books by Graham Oakley) and Marble (named after cake). Sammy was obsessed with mushrooms. He would steal them from the kitchen table—a paw would appear and whisk the mushroom away. Then he'd go crazy chasing the mushroom around the kitchen, until he'd shredded it, leaving a small pile of slimy mushroom pieces for us to step on. I've never met another cat who does this.

HOLLY WEBB

Holly Webb started out as a children's book editor, and wrote her first series for the publisher she worked for. She has been writing ever since, with more than 100 books to her name. Holly lives in England with her husband, three young sons, and several cats who are always nosing around when she is trying to type on her laptop.

For more information about Holly Webb visit:

www.holly-webb.com
www.tigertalesbooks.com